Library of Lessons & Lies

By T. Kulp

Bibliophiles

Book 1

ISBN: 978-1-956612-12-7 (Paperback)
ISBN: 978-1-956612-13-4 (eBook)

This novel is entirely a work of fiction. The names, characters and incidents portrayed in it are the work of the author's imagination. Any resemblance to actual persons, living or dead, events or localities is entirely coincidental.

T. Kulp asserts the moral right to be identified as the author of this work.

Find more stories at https://timkulp.com

First printing edition 2023

Making Adventure Publishing
16944 York Rd, Suite 62
Monkton, MD 21111

To Chris,
seeker of knowledge.

To Greg,
seeker of truth.

To Jasmine,
seeker of things
never found.

"Every worthy act is difficult.

Ascent is always difficult.

Descent is easy and often slippery."

Mahatma Gandhi

Contents

Introduction

Some stories just don't leave you. The first version of this book was written in 1997-ish and began life as a short story. While the original story didn't get the grade I hoped for in my creative writing class, the story wouldn't leave me.

Some things have changed in the story since then. The main character shifted from the professor to the student. The library that starts the book was originally a bookstore. And what happens beyond chapter 3…well, that's all new.

Bookstores and libraries have always held a special place in my heart. I love to get lost in them because you never know what you'll find. The books aren't the only thing I enjoy about these places. I also love the architecture, the design of the shelves, reading spaces, hidden places to read books you don't want to be seen reading. As a kid I spent a lot of time in my hometown library reading books on magic, games, religion, and this trend just amplified in college. Even now it is a common activity for me to go wander around libraries and bookstores just enjoying being there.

There's a common link in horror between places of knowledge (like libraries) and exploring things that perhaps humanity should not know. Cosmic horror's theme of the Curse of Knowledge really resonates with me now more than ever. In the internet age we all are learning that knowledge can be weaponized and turned against us. Misinformation, disinformation, 'fake news,' social networks, and the constant churn of 24-hour news outlets have drowned us in knowledge without the context or social antibodies to know how to deal with this new reality of life. We don't need Lovecraftian monsters terrorizing us with what we know; we have the omnipresent internet to do that.

Manipulation of information and trust in the source are the easy topics of this book. There are more challenging things facing our characters and all of us in life.

Coupling information and addiction was clear to me as I see people who cannot tear away from their phones. Getting every tweet, being sucked into every new post in their feed, seeing the up-to-the-moment information flooding our world – it all reminds me of too many people who just wanted one more drink, one more hit, one more whatever it was in the moment. Our devices bring out our inner addicts and the companies who do that are rewarded with advertising revenue, investment dollars, and the status we grant to the apps that integrate into our lives.

This book is a part of a much larger story. If you read my other books you might find familiar faces, familiar places, familiar situations. If you have not read BLOTS or [dis]connection, I would encourage you to do so. I'm hopeful that you'll be delighted in the connections you find along the way.

One final note: Remember to always question the source when seeking knowledge. Beware what you see online or even in books. Not all books have your best intentions in mind, but this one does. You can trust this book. Honest…

T. Kulp

Baltimore, MD

April 7, 2022

September
2010

Richardsport, PA

Infection

Dr. Gregory Roderick

Curson Street Shadows

Is this the place?

Fighting to straighten Russ's note,
the howling winds
trying to rip it away.

I read the scrawled letters
scribbled together
in a single madman's thought:
700 Curson Street.

Golden light flickers and
sputters in the dusk twilight.
Above the white wooden door
a sign reads Snow Library.

Cold gusts puff out
from the cracked open door
a sliver of dark
whistling winter air
into the warm night.

On the door,
grimy brass numbers
list the address:
700 Curson Street.

I stuff Russ's note into my sport coat,
the navy blue pocket hard to find
in the shadows swimming around me.

All the streetlights are out
with only the stars glaring down.
Watching me,
egging me on
to claim what
Russ left me
on the library counter.

Through the open door
I see the library is dark.
Dim starlight isn't enough
to show anything beyond
the white door.

Stepping up the concrete stairs
I touch the brass door handle,
hinges whisper their invitation
as the door floats open.

Russ's note said to go in
no matter what.
But did he mean
no matter

how bad the feeling
in my gut is

or

how my note looks like it was
written after a psychotic break.

Go in.
No matter what.

My situation becomes clear
as I peek in the door
seeing shadow,
reminding myself
the door is open.

This isn't breaking and entering.
This isn't suspicious.

I'm just checking
to see...
to see what?

If everyone is okay?
Why the door was open?

No, I'm here
because of the book.

Russ said it was here.

I need it.

After all these years
a little breaking and entering
isn't going to stop me
from discovering the
truth.

Inside Snow Library

My eyes adjust quickly
to the lightless library.

Wavering pillars of books emerge
from the sea of shadows.
Not shelves but pillars
piled high in stacks
from the floor to my shoulders.

Towers of piles,
mountains of mounds
spot the floor,
creating a forest of
hiding spots for anyone
sneaking through this library
at night.

Russ's note said
the book is on the counter.

The dark oak counter
that rises from the darkness
is empty.

Not even a bell or a check-out machine.

The shelves match the counter,
all dark oak with
flourishes curling
into spirals
and adornment.

All the shelves are empty.
Books moved from the shelves
to the pillars...
pillars that wave like seaweed
in the current of cold air and shadow.
Pillars reaching toward me.

But the books aren't moving...
it's just the light in here
or the lack of light
playing tricks.

The number of pillars and piles
is just surprising.
Wherever that breeze is coming from
is making me think
they're moving.

I laugh at myself
for getting so worked up.

On the gray carpet in front of the counter
a folded paper flaps in the wind.

Bending down, my knees pop,
echoing through the first floor
like cracking twigs in a forest
alerting predators to my presence.

And like a deer in those woods,
I freeze
to scan my surroundings.

Is there a night guard?
I didn't even think
about that.

Nothing answers
my knees' pop
except another
gust of frozen air
drifting from...
outside, I guess?

Staying down,
I pick up the new note
on the floor and open it.

Another note from Russ,
but not as panicked.
Written while his sanity
was still intact.

Take it to the Vault?
Mike's bar?
Mike said Russ was
coming back later.
Perhaps we're going to talk about it?

A sign on the far wall
emerges from the gloom:
No fiction here. Only knowledge.

I'll need to come back to browse.

A cool draft comes again
bringing my neck hairs to attention.
My head snaps to the origin;
the basement door is cracked.

Must be a draft.
The mystery of the cold breeze
is solved.
I laugh to myself again.

As my eyes adjust,
seeing deeper into the
darkness enveloping me,
the brass railing of a
spiraling staircase
appears.

The staircase
goes up.

I step through the mounds of books
spotting the floor.
Checking behind each piled tower
for anyone waiting to snatch me
into the unnatural darkness that lingers
just beyond the light outside.

Reaching the staircase I pause
at the sign:

Employees Only

A yellow rubber-coated chain
holds the sign across the stairs.
My hand goes to the chain clasp
and I pause.

My eyes drift back to the door
then to the stairs
and the sign.

Turn back?

Is this what a tenured professor
should be doing?
Creeping around an empty,
closed library at night
for a book?

For a book
that I've been searching years for.
For a book
that doesn't exist, according to my peers.

What if I came back tomorrow?

No, I can't.

The sign outside
said the library is closed
for repairs.

Tomorrow the doors might be locked.
Why weren't they locked tonight?

My mind returns to the stairs
and I discover the chain, disconnected,
resting on the floor.

My hands doing things
that my mind hasn't yet
consciously approved?

Walking up the wooden stairs
I take care to stay on the thin
red runner that flows up
to the second floor.

Curving with the staircase,
I follow the twisting climb
to the second floor
to find seven shelves
spanning floor to ceiling.

At the end of each shelf
is a clock with no numbers.
All the clocks are set to midnight
except the last two.

One says three o'clock,
another says 8:30.

Checking my watch,
it's 9:12pm.

CLICK

My muscles lock in place as
I listen down the stairs.

What was that click?

It sounded like a deadbolt locking...

Footsteps follow.
Thick boots,
work boots,
clop across the wooden floor downstairs.

A wellspring of sweat
seeps down my lower back
catching the chill of that
basement breeze...

The first step
of the staircase creeks.
Two sets of boots
stomp up the stairs
and they're not trying to be quiet.

Pursuit

No sense in me being quiet either.

Outside the large windows
the moon pushes through clouds
throwing its pale blue glow
into the second floor of the
lightless library.

I run to the second bookcase.
Rushing down the aisle
to the book sticking out
on the third shelf.

Grabbing it
I stop
and feel the vibration warbling down my spine,
burning off the cold sweat
with the heat of deep yearning.

This is it.

The cover –
worn, thinned brown leather.
The spine –
broken and stretched.

I flip open the cover
and see the title.
It slips from my mouth
in a gasping breath that
exhales the sweetness of discovery.

The Garden and the Well...

It's real.

It's here.

I have it now.

The spine creeks open,
sighing relief.
Relief that it finally found me.

I echo the sigh
with a moan of
anticipation.

Feeling the book,
a whisper comes to my mind;
a delighted chuckle,
disquieting at first
dissolving to

calming.

Boots pound up the stairs
bringing me back to now.
I look down the aisle,
seeing a hallway.

Sprinting to it, I look to the windows.
Moonlight casting long deep shadows
in slices through the second floor.

A fire escape must be here somewhere.

At the end of the hall,
a metal staircase goes up to another floor.
I could hide there...
but they'd find me.

Who are They?

Does it matter?
Tenure or not,
it won't look good for my career
if I'm arrested here...
or mugged...
or killed?

The boots hit
the hard wood of
the second floor.

They are here.

I back up against a shelf.
Silencing my breathing.

My heart is beating too loud.
They will feel it through the floor,
through the shelves.

The window at the end of the hall.
I see it now, and the fire escape.

I slowly draw in a breath;
I'm not a runner
but I can move between the shelves,
stick to the slashes of darkness
cast by the moonlight
and get out before they notice.

Looking around the shelf,
I see one of them.

Stocking cap,
chiseled face,
bone-breaking knuckles,
head-crushing hands.

I move quickly to the next shelf
and don't hear anything.
Looking,
seeing I'm clear,
I move again.

Reaching the window,
I open it slowly
and an idea comes to me.

I grab a book from the shelf beside the window
throw it out the window.

CLANG! CLANG CLANG
as the book falls down the stairs.

I walk with fast exaggerated steps
up the aisle,
then head back to the stairs
while the boots rush toward the window.

My pulse pounding
my blood rushing
I sprint as silently as possible
down to the first floor
of the library.

Book in hand
I burst into the dark
of Curson Street.

Stomping steps bark behind me
as the work boots get closer.
They were not distracted long.

Don't look back.
Keep running.

I get to the corner
and don't stop,
turning almost tripping
on Ross Street.

Frozen lungs scream to slow down
to return to a walk but
the boots scream louder
chasing me to the water taxi
waiting at the edge of the harbor for
tonight's tourists and bar flies.

Jumping onto the boat,
cradling my book
I look around and see two figures
stopping in the shadows.

They don't come into the light,
don't come near the water taxi.

I laugh as we pull away.
Other people in the boat
shift away from me.
Repelled by the sweat
flooding out of me
or the stink of someone
who just ran in a sport coat
and jeans on a cool fall night.

Or perhaps repelled
by the pure glee
boiling inside me,
bursting through my smile.

I sigh
deep,
cleansing.

Finally.

It's mine.

I've found it.

I can show the others,
my peers, that
I'm not crazy,
I didn't make all this up,
this is the proof.

The Garden and The Well.

I

The Seeker

Chapter 1

Beatrix Clark

The Call

Brrr...

Brrr...

"Hello?"

I inhale the
smell of lavender
from my candle.

Letting the relaxing scent
settle on me before I begin.

"Hi Mom."

"Oh, hi,"
Mom says.
She just woke up.
"Isn't it early for a call?"

I look outside
at the people milling about.
Everyone heading to
their first class
of the morning.

9am class.

"No Mom. It's about 9am."

Sometimes I forget
that home is in the same time zone
as Richardsport
because Kentucky seems
a world away from here.

This place is the big city
compared to home,
but only compared to home.
Pittsburg is a few hours away
and that would make Mom's
Kentucky
horse country
mind explode.

"Oh, yeah. It is.
Guess I slept in.
Why are you calling?"
Her mattress springs creak
as she rolls over in bed.

I look to my calendar
seeing the screaming red X
on today's date.

"Just checking in."

Silence on the line.
Is she thinking about what today is?
Did she remember this year?
How could she forget?
My hand drifts to the deck of cards
on my desk but I snatch it back
to my jeans,
wiping off the sweat.

"So, doing anything today
or just going
back to sleep?"
I blow out my candle,
feeling the need for calming scents
has passed.

                              "Yeah. I think I will."
                              She sighs.
                              Her mattress squeaks
                              and whines as she settles
                              back down.

"Okay."
My eyes drift back
to the calendar,
I wonder what else
I should say.

"Okay. Bye Beatrix,"
Mom says.

Click.

I nod.

On my desk
the cards wait
for me to recognize them.

Their dark gray backs
worn and arched from
too many flips.

My hand drifts to them,
knocking on the deck before I can
pull away.

Deep breath. I reach for the top card
but the calendar
steals my attention again,
and I freeze before plucking a card.

I put my phone on the deck.

Maybe the weight
will flatten them out
today.

Maybe it will remove the curl
from my recent overuse.
Too many draws lately making
no sense.
Too many readings leaving me
with more questions
than answers.

Unlocking my door,
I grab my bookbag
and head to Anthropology.

Pausing,
checking to see
The Roommate's door still shut.

I tiptoe past the
eye-searing orange door
trying not to make a breeze and
flutter the photo booth strips
and affirmative sayings.

I open my mind
to see if she's still in there.
Listening for any sign of her,
hearing her thoughts.

This lighting sucks,
she thinks.

Probably posting to her
SocialNet feed again.
Shaking away the stupidity of that,
I sneak down the stairs
and out the door
unnoticed.

I guess today
could have started out
worse than it did.

Anthropology

Ugh...
The desks are in
a circle
again.

Discussion class.
I get to hear
the deep thoughts of
the cheerleaders
and football players
who didn't do the reading
and just keep talking
until Dr. Roderick tells them
to stop trying.

Why bother?

They didn't do the work.
They just pretend
all the way through life.
And people let them.

Why does Dr. Roderick
set up classes like this?

The other students fill in,
keeping their distance
as the last seats to be taken
are those next to me.

Dr. Roderick comes in
with his academia issue
tweed sport coat,
beat-up jeans,
scraggly hair.

"Good morning class,"
he exclaims,
too chipper
for this early.

No one responds.
They continue their discussions
around me.
Ignoring him.

"Okay, let's get to it then.
Count off one through five."
He points to the first in the circle.

"One,"
she grumbles.

"Two,"
next person mumbles.

The count continues
resetting at five.
I sink in my chair
seeing the start of something
coming toward me.

The wave of numbers,
coming at me fast
in pulses of one through five.

Building higher and higher
my nerves tingling with
the realization
that I'm number
three.

A group project is coming.

I look to the other threes.
There is a collective eye roll
when I say three.

The moment they learned I was in their group,
each of them wished to be another number.
And I feel the same.

I want to be number six.

The only six.

       "Your groups are assigned.
       Your project is to
       answer the following question:
       What does it mean to be human?"

       He writes it on the chalkboard
       and underlines it in his usual
       flourish.

       "Get together now and discuss.
       I expect a paper with citations
       and original thoughts..."
       He looks to the
       cluster of frat boys,
       emphasis on 'original.'
       "...by next week."

As the chaos of class rearranging starts
I go to Dr. Roderick.
"I think I'd be better
alone on this project,
Dr. Roderick."

The other threes nod
behind me.

                              Dr. Roderick smiles
                              and shakes his head.
                              "Not again Beatrix."

"I work better alone."
I prepare my hand
for the counting of reasons
having memorized them
for such occasions
throughout my academic career.

"One-"

                              "No chance."
                              He looks at me
                              with those almost-black eyes.
                              Flecks of gold spatter
                              around his iris.
                              "You need to experience
                              working with a team.

                              Can't do everything alone."

"But-"

                              "No."

He erases his flourish
sending a smoky cloud
wisping around us.
"You need to trust others
to do their part
and they need to trust
you will do yours."

"But...they won't do
good work. They'll just
slack off and I'll
have to do everything."

Ugh, what a bitch,
thinks one of the threes.

I round on him
and his stupid spiky hair.
"You don't even know
the half of it!"

He looks surprised
and I turn back to
Dr. Roderick.

Gotta be more
careful.

That wasn't smart.

"Please reconsider?"

He looks at the threes
and they all nod,
eager to get rid of me.
"Work together.
Your grade is on the line."

He strides off
to group one
and starts talking.

Defeated
I plop down in
a group three chair
and listen to their stupid ideas.

Spiky hair
looks at me
with caution.

I crinkle my nose
and give him my
go-away eyes.

He looks to the group
and stays quiet
the rest of the class.

Claudia Bain

The Roommate

My shot is framed.

Mr. Baggins the bear
is angled right.
The pillowcase is flattened
but its lime green color
casts a sickly shine
on my cheeks.

This lighting sucks.

Pulling my ring light closer
I see the sickly look
fade away.

Oh, crap.

The Johnson Snowboard poster
is out of the shot.
I shimmy over a bit,
pulling the ring light
to balance the lighting.

Okay, now.

CLICK.

Quickly typing:

"Woke up like this.
What you doin?"

Emojis.

Post.

Sitting up
tossing my phone down
I throw on a sweater
to cover up this
too-tight tank top
and peek out my door.

The Roommate is gone.

I listen
waiting to hear
someone downstairs.

My phone dings with someone
responding to my post.
I roll my eyes and wonder
who believes this shit.

The Roommate is gone. No sign.

"It's for her own good,"
I whisper to myself
and knock on her
barren white door.

It opens.

Peeking in
smiling;
seeing she's gone
I listen again.

Nothing but SocialNet alerts.
Likes and comments of others
who 'woke up this way.'

I go in
and check the usual
stash spots.

Under the mattress,
sock drawer,
in the leg of the chair,
under the desk.

Nothing.

Then what's she doing in here
all the time?

I pick up her phone
and look at the standard lock screen.
No personalization.
Swiping up
the phone opens.

Who doesn't lock their phone?

Someone with nothing to hide?
Or someone who's an expert
at hiding.

Under the phone
gray cards with gold line art
shift out of their
perfect alignment.

"Shoot."
I straighten them,
feeling the bend.

Perhaps she's a poker shark?

I peel up
the first card.
It slides up easy
almost jumping into my hand.

It's a tarot card.
Nine swords line a wall
while a man cries.

Weird.

I pull up the next card.

It's the same.

The next.

Same.

All the cards
are the same.

I pile them back up
straightening the stack
placing her phone
on top.

In her room,
the gray walls
the bleach white blanket
the desk,
everything the definition
of spartan.

Only a few candles
and a calendar are here
for decoration.

The smell of lavender
is nice
and faint.

Not the
cover-something-up smell
I was expecting.

A red X is on today's date.
September 19th.
A note under it,
'Call Mom first thing'

What's special about today?

Bed unmade.

Candles mostly melted.

Books piled up.
No bookshelves, just piles of books
scattered over the floor.

This must have been
what was in all those boxes
on moving day.

Books on witchcraft,
ancient civilizations,
world religions,
electrical engineering...

"One of these is not like the others..."

The books on witchcraft are old,
tattered and well-read
with spines showing their
frequent use.

Knocking on the apartment door.

                    "Hey C!"
                    It's Quinn.
                    "Class time, girl!"

I step out of
The Roommate's room
and crack the door
back to where it was.

"Be down in a sec!"

It's for her own good.

I ditch my sweater
and pull on the jeans
I'm scheduled to wear today.

Too many holes for me
and today's the last day
I have to wear them
unless the sponsorship contract
updates and I hope to god that doesn't happen.

Today's too-tight outfit
sponsored by C&M, making useless clothes
since 1974.

I kiss my fingers
putting them on my sister's picture
letting them linger
as I look back to The Roommate's room.

Beatrix's room.

I'll check on her later.

Beatrix Clark

The Circuit

Forgot my textbook.

I'll just look at
another book
and pretend
to follow
along.

On the board
the professor draws
a circle with a + and – sign.

A line snakes around
to a squiggly line
to an arrow
back to the circle.

"A circuit..."
His finger traces the line.
"...is like a river."
His voice hits the
boredom-invoking monotone
that only professors can
tap into.

"Hey, you wanna share
my book?"
The boy beside me leans over.
"I know some of this already."

I shake my head
and keep my eyes
in my book.

"I don't mind. Really."
He puts his book on my desk
as the professor keeps
talking about the river
of electricity.

"No thanks."
I give it back to him.

His thoughts come fast,
screaming into my mind.

Why?
She's cute.
It's her hair.
Purple hair is hot.
Maybe she's not into guys?

Just take my book before
the professor notices.
I'm screwing this up.
Say something funny.
Maybe she'd like to see a movie?

"I'm good."
I nod firm.
"Seriously.
Thank you."

Returning to my book
I smell an electrical burn
and look up
to the plume of smoke
streaming from the professor's desk.

"And that's how you
short circuit a circuit."
He holds up a burnt metal wire.
"You create a loop for the river
using a more conductive material
and that amplifies the current.
Short circuits are no fun.

Just ask a kid who sticks a knife
in a toaster."

The class laughs.

The boy beside me smiles
and nods to me.

"That was not a joke,"
the teacher grumbles,
frustrated,
but his voice can't get out
of his monotone.

The boy is cute.

The electrical stink
clings to my nose
as I listen for more thoughts.

Everyone is thinking
about the smell.
But not for long.

Someone is thinking about their
girlfriend.
Someone else is thinking about someone
they wish was their girlfriend.

Someone else is wondering
if they're pregnant.

No one is thinking about
short circuits.

I take a breath and focus
on keeping the voices out.
In my mind I picture building a wall
brick by brick to block out their thoughts.

Quiet comes slowly.
The boy beside me is still
looking at me.
I shift away and put my book
between us.

Books

My book cart is full
and ready for reshelving.
I push it to the elevator
and go down
to the bottom floor.

Religion and Occult.

Some of the books
on my cart
belong there,
some don't,
but that's where
I want to be.

I'm not paid by the book
just the time I put in.

Productivity is not
a metric Arbor University
cares about.

The cart sits full
at the end of the
shelves ending in
the 100s and 200s.

I look for recent
additions.
Donations from some family,
a label in the books that says: Rylan Family.

New books are easy to find.

They break the familiar feel
of the spines
as my fingertips glide
over the shelves.

New books make new dips
or textures or bulges
where they were not before.

A few books look promising.

A book on
witchcraft in the 19th century.
Stories of people drinking
ground-up mummies
as a magical potion.

Sounds gross.

Stories about
old grandmothers in Appalachia
who could grow things when others couldn't,
who were midwives helping their communities,
who

knew things.

A story catches my eye:
The Ghost of the Mountain.
It starts off with a death
as many ghost stories do,
and talks about how the ghost
met a woman who didn't know
she was a witch.

The woman learned of her power
as she wandered the mountain
with the ghost.

> "Cart won't empty itself,"
> Margaret grumbled.

"Don't you have
a computer to fix or something?"

I scoff her away.

She returns the scoff
and moves on.

Probably back to the computer lab
to sit and wait for someone
to forget their password.

Returning to the book,
it describes the woman
who became a witch
as a kind person.

A beautiful person.

How unusual.
Normally, witches are portrayed
as monsters,

and they are.

They buck the order
of the patriarchy
and don't need anyone
to provide for them.

They don't need anyone.

They know
everyone leaves.

So, they read
and study
and stay to themselves.

Trusting in their books
and lessons to give answers
and help when needed.

Don't expect anyone else
to do anything
but burn you
at the stake.

I put the book back,
feeling the
six-petal rose emblem
on the spine.
The dulled gold leafing
still catches some light
but it needs a shine.

Going back to my cart,
I look for 100s
and stuff them
into their numbered places.

Bringing order
to this chaos.

Dinner

Opening the apartment door
I peek in, seeing no sign
of The Roommate.

Claudia.

All clear.
I head to the kitchen
and pull out a pot for
mac and cheese.

Start the water,
collect supplies
to make this a fast dinner.

Claudia's fine,
just not my type of person.
She's all about being
popular
and wants
everyone
to like her.

She'd probably be posting
on SocialNet
how mac and cheese is made.
Emojis and likes
flying around.
Gibberish comments
LOL
AF
whatever else
is on there.

"Hey,"
Claudia says.
Her excitement
matching her online persona.

Startled
I didn't feel her
come in.

I smile and nod
quickly returning to my
mac and cheese boiling water.

"Wow, I didn't know
you still lived here."
She chuckles
and leans on the counter.

"Just like to keep
to myself."
My books are better company
than most people.
Learning,
growing my abilities,
that wall thing was a recent find,
and every moment I talk to Claudia
is a moment I'm not learning,
not improving.

"I'm going to have
some friends over tonight,"
she says.

"I'll stay in my room,"

I agree before she asks.
Works for me.

> "Oh, no."
> She goes to the fridge
> opening the door.
> "If you'd like to join us
> I'd love that."
> She pulls out the mayonnaise.
>
> Scooping some into a measuring cup
> she puts the heaping white glob
> beside my pot.

"I'm busy tonight."
The mayonnaise chunks over the rim
and drips onto the counter.

> "If you change your mind
> we'll be down here."
> She points to the mayonnaise.
> "Makes more creamy
> mac and cheese.
> Use that instead of butter."

How would she know?

Models don't eat this kind of stuff.

Pretty girls with
thousands of followers
don't eat mac and cheese
like the rest of us.

A chunk of mayonnaise
falls to the counter
and I shiver at thought of
ruining my mac and cheese.

I pick up the butter
and say,
"No thanks."

Claudia nods
and pulls out the scrunchy
that was binding her silky black curls.

"Don't know what you're missing."
She smiles and puts
the mayonnaise back.
"I'll check in
when people get here."

"No need."
I drain the water,
letting the steam
hide me for a moment.

She goes upstairs
in her cheery
hippity-hop step.

Her thoughts go instantly to
setting up a post for SocialNet.
Yeah, that's more her speed.

Mixing it all together,
the butter,
the cheese sauce,
the milk.

The mayonnaise sits
globbed and goopy
in the measuring cup.

I'm not cleaning that up.

Claudia Bain

Invitation

My phone buzzes
with the latest comment
on the chip bowl picture
I posted
for the party.

Food posts always do well
and Doritos are a
crowd favorite online.

Makes sense.
Who doesn't love Doritos?

Tucking my phone away
in my back pocket,
I knock on Beatrix's
barren door.

No signs,
no pictures,
nothing but blankness.

But that can't be who she is.
Her purple hair,
nice clothes – not brand name
but not ripped and worn,
she takes care of herself
but isn't vain or obsessive.

She doesn't seem like someone
with no one.

"I'm busy,"
she calls out.

Sounds like she's at
her desk.

"Can I come in?"
I ask.

She doesn't answer.
Wouldn't have mattered if she did.
I'd still do what I'm doing,
turning the doorknob
and slowly opening the door.

I peek in a bit.
"Hi. Can I come in?"

She's at her desk
and doesn't turn
but I think I hear
an eye roll.

"You don't have to come down,
but we've lived together
for like a month
and I barely know you."
I sit on her bed.
It squeaks.

"I mean, I know you like to read."
I point to the stacks of books,
scanning for topics:
witchcraft, occult,
the aberrant electrical engineering textbook.

She snickers a laugh.

"What?"

"No, nothing."
She pages through a book
on her desk.

A spring is poking me
through the blankets.
How does she sleep on this?
I'm thankful my mom pushed me
to get the new mattress.

Seeing the red X on her calendar
I try to make a connection.
"The party could be for
whatever's special about today?"

I point to the calendar.
She freezes at that
locking in place.

"Or...not. Sorry.
I just thought that might be
something special."

"It is,"
she grumbles,
more sad than
angry.

"I'm sorry.
I didn't mean to..."

"No, you didn't know."
She looks at the door
inviting me to leave
with her eyes.

What am I doing wrong here?
Changing my approach...

"Is it me?"
I scoot closer to her.
"Was it the mayonnaise?"
I smile.

I think she does too.

"I'm not a people person,"
she says.

Moving closer
she slides her tarot cards
into her deck and
turns them over.

The gray backs and gold lines
glitter in the light
of her lavender candle.

"You don't have to be."
My phone buzzes again
and she smirks.

                              "You sure are,"
                              she says.

A trail of smoke
drifts up from her candle
taking the relaxing lavender scent
up to my nose.

I drag in the scent
and think about
Mom and my
aromatherapy sessions
in Los Angeles.

Lavender was always used
to bring us back
to calm after
talking about
Jasmine.

The smell reminds me
of Mom crying.

Beatrix blows out the candle
then blows the smoke away
looking sheepishly back
to her book.

She works hard to avoid
eye contact.
Weird...

"Maybe you don't know me
as well as you think."
I tap her shoulder
with my knuckles.

"Your hair is going to be
the talk of the night."
I point to her
straight purple hair.
White roots are starting to peek out.
"It's awesome."

She smiles.
Wow! A real smile.

My phone buzzes again.

"What do people even say
on your posts?"
She looks at the phone, curious.

"Come downstairs
and I'll show you."
I reach out for her
to take my hand.
"If you don't want to stay
you don't have to."

She looks at me,
looking over the ripped jeans
and tank top.

She's checking my makeup
and nails.

"What?"
I push out a smile
but I know what.
She's judging my costume.

Maybe wondering
if she'll fit in.
She won't.

But I need someone
who doesn't fit in
so I can have a little
escape.
Someone to
escape
with.

"Okay."
She scoops up the cards
on her table.
The deck of just one card.
Weird.

She smiles.
"But just for a bit."

My phone buzzes
and I pull it out
to show her what people post
as we go downstairs.

She chuckles at the
inane and empty comments,
asking why people share
this stuff.

"Not on SocialNet?"

A new alert pops up
of some guy sending me
a picture of his bank account.
Like that's supposed to
impress me.

I shake my head
and chuckle.

            "I don't need a website
            showing me creepy people.
            I do just fine finding
            them myself,"
            she sneers.

            "One time..."
            She pauses,
            smiles wily.
            "...I met a real creeper
            at a con."
            Her nose scrunches up
            with a body trembling shiver.
            "He wanted me to cosplay
            as Slave Laia."
            Her tongue pops out to yack.
            "He had the Jabba part down."

I laugh.
Smiling, remembering
the dread I felt when
I learned I was going to have
a roommate.
The dread of having to perform
at all times.
To always be
Claudia Bain, SocialNet influencer.

When she didn't know
who I was
on move-in day
I was so
thankful.

The pretending could stop
at the door
with her
as my
roommate.

But tonight,
I need to be in
character.

She laughs at
a comment of all
emojis.

"What does this even mean?"
she scoffs.

Maybe I don't
need to be
in character
all night
after all.

Having her here
is going to
make an
interesting
evening.

"Wait...what's a 'con'?"

She looks at me,
cocks an eyebrow,
and laughs.
"Nerd party.
Where you dress up
like your favorite
characters."

I nod
and laugh.

She smiles.

The Party

Beatrix sits on the couch
flipping over the top card
in her deck.

She looks at it.

Puts it
in the middle of the deck,
flips the next.

I guess it's a tick?
Like, how she handles
social anxiety?

People are coming in now
and no one goes near her.

They can sense she's different.

Scared to reach out
to her.

"Hey, want some?"
I hold out a bowl to her.

She looks at it;
recoils.

                              "Mac and cheese?"
                              She grimaces.
                              "Mayonnaise?"

I nod
and hand her a spoon.

"Come on."
She shakes her head
vigorously.

Her eyes lock beyond the spoon
swaying with mac and cheese
fixating on my bracelet.
Puzzled eyes assessing it.
"Gift from my grandma
back home."

                              "In LA?"
                              she asks.

"In Mexico. She didn't move
when my parents
came up here."
I let my fingers wander through
the mountains and valleys of beads
and knotted rope.

"It reminds me of her.
My sister and I..."
Pausing, remembering Jasmine.
"...we use to call Grandma
'Susurra' cause
she whispered everything."

"Looks like an eye."
Beatrix cocks her head.
"Like, the beads around that black
stone
are an eye with lots of different colors
in the iris."

Beatrix looks harder,
straining to see something
so I hold it closer for her
to get a look.

She backs away
as I extend it,
sweat beading up
on her forehead.

Her eyes look to me,
mouth open
forming a
question.

"Hey C!"
Quinn comes up behind me.
I heard her over the music
in those clacking heels.
"What's up here?
Is that mac and cheese?"

"This is my roommate
Beatrix."

I point the spoon to Beatrix,
pulling back my bracelet,
and then scoop up some
mac and cheese.
"She's a mac and cheese purist."

Quinn and her twin -
I don't remember her name -
laugh on queue.

         "Pic with the M&C?
         I didn't know you were so...
         free with your diet!"
         Quinn positions her phone
         in the default
         selfie arm position.

Her lips pucker.
I push in and match her,
holding up the spoon
for the camera.

She snaps the picture
and rushes to type in a caption.

         "M&C with @ClaudiaciousBain!
         #bestlife."
         She hits send
         and the chorus of buzzing starts
         as each phone,
         already in everyone's hands,
         gets the post.

They all like
and comment.

Has Quinn ever eaten mac and cheese?

Is that on the approved food list
from whatever the latest fad diet is?
Nothing wrong with diets,
nothing wrong with Quinn,
just funny that mac and cheese is cool now
because I have it.

A benefit from taking over Jasmine's
SocialNet account I guess.
Inherited awesomeness.

If I had a shit pie
that would be cool too.

Beatrix laughs.
I look to her;
she shakes her head,
looking to her cards.

Quinn shoves the picture under my nose
and I chuckle
seeing what no one else noticed:
Beatrix rolling her eyes
in the background.

Looking to Beatrix,
she gives me an
'are we done now'
look.

"Whoa are those
tarot cards?"
Quinn says.

Beatrix puts the cards
in her pocket.

"Are you like into
that stuff?"
Quinn gets excited
and looks to me for
answers.
"Can she read fortunes?"

I motion to Beatrix
and eat the mac and cheese.
I shrug.
"Ask her."

"Please do me,"
Quinn says sitting beside
Beatrix.

"I don't know if that's
a good idea."
Beatrix shifts and
finds a chip of paint
on the wall much more interesting
to focus on.

Scooping another spoon
of mac and cheese
I watch,
pulling the spoon
through my teeth.

"Up to you Beatrix,"
I say mid-chew.

She looks at me
confirming
and I shrug again.

"Don't blame the messenger."
Beatrix sighs.

Quinn squeals
and claps
as she hugs
Beatrix.

Beatrix snaps away
at the touch of another
human.

Quinn bounces on the couch
watching Beatrix put the
cards on the
coffee table
in front of them.

Around the cards,
cups sweat rings onto
the table Mom picked out
when we moved here.

I want to yell for everyone
to get coasters,
to keep their sweaty drinks
from staining the table
but that's not something
the Claudia Bain
these people know
would do.

So, I lean against the wall,
stepping back to take in
the scene.

Ignoring Mom's future comments
chastising me for not taking care
of the things she works hard to provide
for me.

I watch
Quinn shiver in
anticipation;
so does Beatrix.

                    "Knock on the deck
                    like you're knocking on
                    a door."
                    Beatrix's breath
                    quickens as she waits
                    for Quinn to knock.

Quinn raps her knuckles
on the cards
and giggles.

I bet this is the distraction thing
that magicians do.
They redirect you
to focus away from where
the actual magic is happening:
their other hand,
a secret pocket,
their sleeve…

                    "Get ready."
                    Quinn hands her phone
                    to her twin.
                    "Get it on video."
                    Quinn waves excitedly
                    at the twin who braces
                    for something amazing.

Beatrix runs her hand
over the top of the cards
and motions for Quinn
to pick up a card.

I smile, knowing the card
will be the only card in the deck.
Nine of Swords.

Quinn flips over the card
and it's blank.

An empty white card face.

I look to Beatrix;
she glances at me,
shrugs.

                              "I guess the spirits
                              didn't want to answer."
                              Beatrix grins.

What?

Where's the Nine of Swords?

My eyes meet
Beatrix's
and she looks back to me
curious.

                              "What?"
                              Quinn pulls the next card
                              in the deck.
                              It's blank.

                              Then the next.

                              It's blank.

"These are all just blank?"
Quinn looks to me
for answers.

I look to Beatrix
wondering what we're seeing.

She switched the cards?

Quinn snaps up the deck
and turns them all over
showing all the cards
as blank.

"That's a lame trick,"
Quinn scoffs.

Beatrix looks to her
and scowls.
"I told you.
The spirits didn't answer."

"It's just a blank deck.
I thought it was magic?"
Pouting,
posing for her camera.

Beatrix's jaw flexes,
teeth grinding at being called out.
Didn't think she'd get so easily
agitated...

She shakes her head,
blows out a grunting sigh
then gathers the cards
and places them in a stack
on the table again.

Beatrix knocks.

Pauses.
Looking at the cards.
Her hand reaching for the top card
stopping,
lingering over the deck,
waiting.
She plucks up the first card.

An angel holds a blazing sword
pointing a finger toward the viewer.
In bold black letters,
the card says:

Judgement.

What?

Quinn erupts in cheers
and squeals.
"Wow! Did you get that!?"
She turns to her twin
who nods.
"Do the next one."

Beatrix hands her the deck
and Quinn flips the next
and the next
and the next
and the next
all are the angels
all are Judgement.

What the hell?

Beatrix sighs
and looks back to the paint chip
while Quinn laughs
and giggles.

Beatrix's teary eyes
are a hard contrast
to Quinn's explosion of glee.

"That was awesome.
Let me see the video."
Quinn takes her phone
and watches, seeing
the trick again.
I watch with her
in slow motion
and zoom around to see
the sleight of hand.

But there wasn't any.

We zoom and pan
looking for the trick.
For the switch.
The moment when the blank deck
was exchanged for the Judgement deck...

But there's nothing.

No trick to be seen.

Either Beatrix
should have her own show in Vegas
or something else is going on here.

Susurra use to say,
'Not everything's a trick'
as she passed coins
through my ears.

The coins would sparkle
and vanish in one ear
and reappear out the other.

Jasmine would laugh
and say, 'Teach me'
but Susurra would just say,
'Not everything
can be taught.
Some things
must be caught.'

Where is the Nine of Swords?

Beatrix looks to me,
a frustrated snort
coming out of her.

                              "That's it.
                              You're now Trixie!"
                              Quinn huddles to Beatrix
                              and takes a selfie with her.

I think Beatrix
just threw up in her mouth
at the idea of being called
Trixie.

>   "Hanging with #trixie!"
>   she types and sends the post.

As phones buzz
other people come over
to see what's going on
but Beatrix's tricks are over
for tonight.

She just stares into the corner
and ignores the laughing
and cheers and awe
and fun around her.

"Who wants to go to the club?"
I shout to pull them away
from her.

Cheers erupt throughout the apartment.

>   "Yeah! Come on Trixie!"
>   Quinn grabs her arm
>   and Beatrix recoils in surprise.
>   "You've gotta come!"

Beatrix shakes her head.
I take another bite of
mac and cheese.

The cards are on the table again
and I wonder what they would say
if I picked them up.

"Come on Beatrix,"
I say and smile.
"It'll be fun
and they aren't going to leave you alone
unless you come along."

Beatrix nods,
rolls her eyes,
and staggers up
to go.

I look back to the cards
and reach toward them.

"Don't."
Beatrix grabs my hand.
"Leave them there.
No more for tonight."
She smiles to cover up
some hurt inside her.

I nod and take my bowl
to the sink.
Quinn sticks to Beatrix
as they go out.

The cards are on the table.

The door closes as the last person
leaves our apartment.

Picking up the deck,
I peel up the top card.
Peeking under it,
seeing the swords,
I let the card's edge go.

It claps down
on the other cards
echoing through the
empty apartment
full of life a moment ago
now abandoned
forgotten
fled.

My stomach twists
and sinks with the weight
of knowing something's going to happen.

Something's going to go
wrong tonight.

It's not the cards,
it's a feeling.
And Susurra always said to
trust those feelings.

Rubbing my bracelet,
smiling at so many memories
of her tonight.
Maybe a trip to see her soon
is in the cards.

Chuckling at the quip,
I stuff the deck into my pocket,
feeling this is important.
Feeling 'Trixie's' tricks aren't
quite done
for tonight.

Chapter 2

This Line Sucks

September nights
are not made for
lines outside.

Back home, September is warm
but up here in the mountains,
fall's almost over,
winter slipping in
with the night.

Not the cool pleasant nights,
no,
bitter and biting frost.

Claudia says this place
is amazing but all I see
is a line wrapping around
the block.

I exhale ice crystals
like a dragon.
Quinn thinks it is amazing
but she thinks everything
is amazing
and worth a SocialNet post.

"Waitin' in line!"
Quinn giggles
and posts to SocialNet.

A few moments later:
"Cold night, hot friends!"
She got me in the photo
for that post.

We just met.
I wouldn't say 'friends.'
I don't think I like her.
Too cheery.

"Claudia, it's freezing out."
My teeth clatter.
"Let's head back."

"Ah, no way Trixie!"
Quinn says.
"We're moving. Just slow line.
The Vault is always packed."
Quinn points up the line
to the bouncer at the door.

He looks half monster.

His neck and shoulders
melt together,
a flat top sticking out
where his head should be.

The bouncer's intimidating look
fades as a man walks up to him.

Wait...

"Dr. Roderick?"
I say.

Claudia huddles to me,
shivering in her
poor outfit choice.

Who wears ripped up jeans
on a night like this?
They don't keep you warm.

Are those jeans a sponsor?
Everyone at Arbor talks about
her SocialNet feed.
Her sponsorships.

"You know the bouncer?"
Claudia says
through chattering teeth.

"No, I know the guy
he's talking to.
That's Dr. Roderick
at our school."
I point to the scraggly haired man
who looks sweaty
and too excited to be
the Dr. Roderick
who made me
stay in group three
earlier today.

"Roderick the Mad?"
Quinn giggles
rolling her eyes
bobbling her head.

"Don't call him that.
He's not crazy,
just eccentric."
And a genius.

"You think he could get us in?"
Claudia cuts in.
A shiver rattles her body
as she rubs her chest
with her hands.

"Maybe."
I watch her.
"Shouldn't you be rubbing
your arms?"

Like cold people do?
They rub their arms,
hold them tight to their body.

                    Claudia shakes her head
                    and smiles.
                    "No. If you want to stay warm
                    you warm your core.
                    Your arms will take care
                    of themselves."
                    She motions to Dr. Roderick.
                    "Get us out of this cold."

                    "I heard he believes in aliens,"
                    Quinn says,
                    scandalized.
                    "Like, he talks to them or
                    something."

"No, Quinn."
I'd grind my teeth
if I could get my teeth to
stop chattering.

I look to Dr. Roderick
shaking the bouncer's hand.

Claudia's friends
start encouraging me to go too
and it is freaking freezing out here.

So, I go.

Dr. Gregory Roderick

Admission

The line wraps the corner
with all the kids
waiting to get in
to the Vault.

A few streets away
I stop to gather myself.
Who waits in a line that wraps
a few streets away from the club?

Students are in that line,
I don't doubt it,
they're here every Friday.

My sweaty face,
wrinkled jacket,
all validate my nickname:
Roderick the Mad.

I know they call me that.
I hear the whispers
and don't mind the students
thinking
I'm a little off.

When my colleagues
call me that,
then I mind.

And they do.

One too many accidental
'reply all' emails
showed me that.

Deep breath.

Pulling in the air from the river
brisk and sharp in early fall.

Calm.

Pulse returning to normal
with the only rapidity being
anticipation
for digging into this book.

The Garden and The Well.

It is in my hand,
the vibration of excitement
still rippling
in my bones.

My feet take me
to the front of the line.
Danny's shaking his head at someone
trying to talk their way in.

"Hey Danny. Mike in?"
Danny's face curls up to a smile
as he sees me.

"Hey Greg! Good ta see ya."
Danny puts his knuckles out,
a battling ram fist.
I knuckle back, careful
not to break my hand on his.
"Mike's in.
Was lookin' for ya earlia.
He'zat the bar. Expectin' ya."

Danny opens the red rope
blocking the door.
I step up
to the sighs and scoffs
of the line.

Danny's face snaps back to
a scowl at the line.
His glare smashes the
sighs and scoffs
to silence.

Ha!
When will these kids learn
it helps to know people?
Especially the owner of the club.

Behind Danny
a chalkboard sign reads
Tonight: Delta Devils
$5 cover

I pull out my wallet
and unravel a five.
Danny waves it away
but I push it toward him.

"For the cover,
just take it."

He chuckles,
shaking his head.

                              "Dr. Roderick!"
                              a girl's voice calls
                              from the line.

                              Danny perks up,
                              serial killer look
                              in full effect.

                              "Dr. Roderick, it's me,
                              Beatrix Clark
                              from class."

She shuffles up to me
her purple hair swaying over a vampiric complexion.
Trailing behind her are three others,
not in my class.

I'm surprised I didn't see her sooner.

She looks like she's ready for a protest
in her army jacket and purple Docs.
A pin on her jacket reads:
Beware: Educated and Empowered.

Her friends -
no, perhaps not,
those with her
don't match her.

The lead,
the one pushing Beatrix forward,
belongs here.

        "We've been waiting all night
        and it's freezing out here.
        Can you help us get in?"
        Beatrix says.
        The words choke out of her.

"Ms. Clark."
I nod to Beatrix.
Danny chuckles.
My eyes meet his in an unspoken ask.
He nods approval and pulls the red rope further.

Red.

Not yellow.

Rope.

Not chain.

I look around for the
shadowy figures.

I listen for
pounding work boots.

I pant,
remembering the run.

"Greg?"
Snapping back to now
feeling Danny's hand
weighing my shoulder down.

His faced concerned.
"Ya good?"

I nod
and smile
and roll my eyes.

Beatrix and crew
are clueless.

Gleeful giggles
erupt behind Beatrix.
She doesn't smile
but her eyes drop to the book
then spring up to mine.

The excited vibrations in my arm
pull toward her.
My fingers slip from the spine
as the book lurches at her,
ripping away from me.
Tightening on the book,
pulling it deeper into me,
clutching it from getting
to her.

Did the book try to jump at her?

No. The vibration is just excitement.
I'm still jumpy from escaping
those thugs.

It's my book.
My proof and
I will be the one
to read it.

          "Thank you,"
          she says
          a hint of apology
          in her smile.

          "Trixie does it again!"
          the lead girl barks out,
          triumphant in her inaction.

The kids begin to walk past Danny.
"Stop."
I point to the sign.
"Nothing's free."

My eyes drift back to Beatrix.
She shrugs and digs out the cash.
Her friends hold back groans.
Danny laughs,
holding out his calloused hand.

Beatrix's eyes drop again to the book
as she hands her five over to Danny.

          Danny points to Beatrix.
          "Smart one."

He points to me
as she walks past.
"Smart ones are trouble.
Stay outta trouble."
Danny's finger wobbles
as he nods his warning.

He smiles and pats my shoulder.
A love tap
that cracks my back.

His smile drops,
his eyes darken
as he returns
to his work.

I cradle the book
tight to my chest
and go in.

The Herald

Dark oak bar,
smoked glass shelves,
teal and magenta lights
throbbing to the beat
of the Delta Devils.

Mike hustles from drink to drink
flipping bottles
pouring arcs of alcohol
that would make any Vegas bartender
proud.

I nod to him.

He sees everything here
as if he were the omniscient God
of this place.

No cameras in the bar.

Mike says he doesn't need them.

He sees everything
through the mirrors lining the walls,
the ceilings,
the tables,
glass surfaces that reflect everything
to everyone.

In the Vault,
you can't hide
what you do or
who you are.
This place sees everyone
in the reflections
everywhere.

Mike nods back
flipping a bottle
holding up a finger to signal
Wait.
Catches the bottle and pours a
golden shot of whiskey.

I sidle to the bar
keeping the book
tucked into my jacket
like a gun.

        "Thank you, Dr. Roderick,"
        an apologetic
        soft
        voice says.

I turn,
it's Beatrix again.
She sits a stool away from me.

        "I didn't want to ask
        but Claudia's friends pushed it."
        She looks to her drink.
        A Sprite with grenadine.

Clever.

        "The bouncer
        wasn't letting anyone in."

"Danny."
I pick up the Jameson
Mike just dropped off.
"You should have talked to him.
You'd like him."

She scoffs.

        "He's more Claudia's type."
        She shakes her head.

"I meant as an academic."
I sip the sweet golden drink.

A slight burns follows it down my throat.
My hand clenches the book tighter.

She saw it.

> "Oh...I didn't think of him
> that way. Looks like
> he'd rather use a book to
> beat someone
> than
> learn something."
> She snickers a laugh.
> A snort slips.

I chuckle too.
"Yeah, I can see that."
Imagining Danny reading a book
then pausing, beating someone with it,
and then reading the rest.

"So, Trixie?"
I chuckle.
"I'm surprised to see
you with other humans."

She rolls her eyes
and shrugs.
Her eyes drop
to the book
again.

> "Was that a book in your hand?"
> She points to my jacket.
> "Leather cover?
> Old?"

My hand retreats further into my jacket.
I lean away.
My arm tenses, holding the book to me,
feeling it pull toward her again.

She leans in,
confusion squinting her eyes;
a question forming.

I shiver and shrug
to break away from her.

Finishing my drink,
turning my eyes to the glass shelves
watching in the reflection
her eyes
greedily glare
into the dark of my jacket.

Another Jameson appears.

"If you'll excuse me."
I stand up
with quick steps to pull away from her.
Her icy blue eyes follow the book.

She follows me
as I head to the stairs
leading to the VIP area.

"Is that the VIP area?"
She looks down
trying to see beyond the stairs.

"VIP sounds so formal.
It's for friends of the bar."
The bouncer, I don't recognize him,
new guy,
looks to Mike
and then
the red rope opens for me.

I walk through.

The rope closes behind me.

I turn, pushing the book deeper
into me and
away from her.

"Have fun tonight but not too much fun.
Class is tomorrow afternoon
and I expect you've done the reading."

I force a smile.

Beatrix Clark

Things I'd Rather Be Doing

"Awwww...you didn't even
get a drink
out of him."

What...?

What was that?
That book...
it...
no.

Imagined voices.
That's all.
It didn't talk to me.

Oh, Claudia's here.
I look to her hand;
she's holding
the same drink
as me.

Sprite with grenadine.

                              "Don't drink either?"
                              Claudia points to my drink.

"I thought you'd be more..."
I wave my drink around.
"...Red Bull and vodka."

She shakes her head
contorting her face
in disgust.

"Don't like to be
out of control,"
she says
and waves me to the bar.

Quinn and the others
are throwing down shots.
Losing control seems to be high
on their list of things to do.
The neon magenta lights
pulse over their white shirts
and white scrunchies.

Clothes designed to light up
in this club.
Claudia and I
disappear in our dark outfits.

We vanish
into the crowd
and reemerge at the bar
forgotten by the party
around us.

"Don't you need to post something?"
I ask
trying not to sound
dismissive.

She sips her drink.
"Just did.
Besides, it's just a job."
Sips again
twirling the stirrer.
"Just doing what's
expected."

Her eyes bulge in a long sigh
but I don't listen to her thoughts.
Some sighs tell you to stay out,
tell you 'I don't want to talk about it'
and that was one.

A dropped glass
shatters the pause between us.

We both look.

Quinn dropped her drink
and her friends laugh
and shout for another
round.

"Why?"
I finally ask her.

I look back to Claudia
seeing her thoughts
of someone...
a girl...

She turns back to me
and shuts me out.
"Why do we do anything?"

Laughing, she leans on the bar.
"Parental expectations."

The spiky hair juggler
comes to us
cleaning a glass
with a white rag
glowing in the teal lights.

"Those your friends?"
he asks,
nodding to Quinn's group.

"Nope."

Claudia shrugs.
"Yeah, sort of."

"Tell them to chill out
or get out before I ask
the bouncers to tell them,"
he says.

Claudia nods
and grins
then walks to Quinn.

They talk
but I can't hear them
over the screaming
from the band.

"You know Greg?"
he says,
pours another drink.

His Hawaiian shirt and khaki shorts
don't really match the
industrial electronic music
grumbling through the bar.

Spiky blonde hair
and thick glasses
looking like he belongs at a
luau with the chess club.

"Dr. Roderick?"
I clarify.

He nods.
"I'm Mike.
You the designated driver?"

He refills my drink.

"No, just don't like-"
Losing control.
"-drinking too much."

Chuckling.
"Hangovers, you know."

That's the safe answer
but the hangover isn't
the worst part.

Drowning in the voices
of others,
their screams,
their crying inside,
being unable to block out
the voices of everyone around you
because you can't focus...

That's the worst part.

I'll take a hangover any day
compared to hearing
everything
everyone
is thinking
at once.

He smiles
and nods.

"You know Dr. Roderick?"
I ask.

> "Yep, Greg and I go
> way back."
> He sweeps up another glass
> and starts another pour.

His eyes jut around
the bar
taking it all in
seeing every half-empty glass,
the pace of sips,
the melting ice.
"He's a good dude.
Sharp as a whip."

"Does he always read here?"
The question slips out;
I didn't know
I wanted to ask.

"Yep.
This one he was all
excited about, so don't expect
to see him again tonight."

Mike starts spinning bottles
and juggling drinks again
like a fluid machine winding up
to full speed.
"Let me know if
you need anything."

Pointing to Quinn.
"That doesn't include
free drinks."
He winks.

I try to laugh away
embarrassed burning cheeks
but I can't.

As Mike walks away
my eyes drift back
to the stairs,
to the book.

What did it say?

I listen,
opening my mind
to hear it.
Focusing on it.

Muffling out the other voices
the drunken thoughts
the wishful thinking
the malicious desires

Come.

The book
grabs my shoulder
pulling me around.

Infiltration

Claudia lets go of
my shoulder.

"You okay!?"
She puffs up
scanning around me.

Protector mode
was triggered
and suddenly she looks
fierce.

Like, stomp someone down
to a bloody mess
fierce.

"I thought I heard…"
My eyes drift to the stairs again
but I don't hear anything.
I don't feel the voice.

She relaxes
as I relax.
"What's the deal
with that guy?"

She motions to the stairs
where Dr. Roderick
went with the
leather cover,
the aged pages.

"He's one of my professors."

"Are you and him…?"
She smiles.

"No!"
I shake
vigorously enough
to convince us both
I'm not interested.

"I mean, he's cute."
She looks to the bar
taking a drink.
"Not judging or anything."
Claudia shakes her head
and shrugs, discarding any idea
that such a relationship
would be wrong.

"No. I'm not like that,"
I say
and she nods
knowingly.
"No, I'm just not
the relationship type."

She shrugs
and accepts the answer.
She should,
it's true.

"Did you see the book
he had?"
I ask.

Claudia pushes up from the bar,
an airy chuckle flowing out.
"Ah, that makes sense.
The book is what you're into."
Nodding as her image of me
is confirmed.

Claudia thinks about
the pile of books
in my room.

She's looking at the piles
then looks around…

          Hello?
          she thinks.

Shaking her head
she comes back to the moment
and gives me a confused look.

Did she notice me
in her mind?

Uneasy quiet
settles between us
pressing down the grinding beat
of the Delta Devils.

          "Not to change topics,
          but how'd you do the card trick?"
          She turns back to the bar
          resting her elbows on the
          hard wood.

"Oh, that's just a…"

          Magic,
          she thinks.

"…just a sleight of hand."
I complete my thought,
ignoring hers.

My eyes drift back
to the stairs.
Trying to see down
but a red curtain
blocks the view.

"Is the book about
magic or occult stuff?"
Claudia asks.

I turn to her
but she's still leaning
on the bar.

She turns to me
and smiles,
expecting an answer.

"I don't know."
I shrug.
"I think so."

I didn't say anything,
she thinks.
Just thought it.

Oh crap.

She smiles
a toothy
gotcha grin.

"Well, let's go find out."
Claudia points to the stairs.

Foiled

"How?"
Dumbfounded
disarmed
she's figured it out.

How is a
SocialNet influencer
the first person
to notice something's
different
about me?

She shouldn't even
notice me.

"I looked at the cards
in your room earlier."
Her eyes apologize
but I don't care.

She was looking for...
drugs in my room.

Not for her.

To stop me from
using them.

The images crash into her mind
as her forehead creases
and she pushes me out.

"Stay out unless I invite you."
Claudia's smile
vanishes in that statement.

She waits for me
to confirm, understanding
that she knows when I'm in there
and to stay out.

I nod
agreeing to her terms.

I've never had
to think about this before.
No one ever notices.

How does she?

"I watched the video of you
and the cards earlier.
You didn't do any
sleight of hand,
and you have a terrible
poker face.

I checked the cards afterwards,
and they were the same as I saw
earlier. The cards changed."
She shakes her head.
"When you eliminate the possible,
whatever remains,
however improbable,
must be the truth."

"Sherlock Holmes?"

"Magic."
Claudia shrugs.
"You or the cards.
I figured it was you
but I wanted to confirm
and just did."

"So, what? You going to post it
on SocialNet?"
I bark at her and
wait to hear her thoughts.
She'll think I'm a freak,
and she's right
then she'll leave.

Claudia laughs.
"Do you try
to push everyone away
this hard?"

I want to push in
and see what she's thinking
but that stare
from moments ago,
the stay out stare,
keeps me away.

"My grandma knew things.
You couldn't ever lie to her
and there were rumors
that she could do...
more."

An old lady handing
Claudia a bracelet
before she came to Richardsport,
the old lady looks to me
shaking her head,
denying me.

The image vanishes.

"Also, my sensei back in LA
has done things with
his Ki energy that…"
She thinks about a time when
he blew out a candle
from across the room
with his Ki energy.
"…just sayin',
reading minds isn't
too much of a jump when you've seen
people shatter concrete with their
head."

Claudia nods to
close the conversation
then turns to the stairs.
"We going to get this book
or what?"

"I don't need help."
Shaking away the thought.

"Of course not."
She starts walking
toward the stairs.
*But I'm going to help
anyway.*

Peeking over her shoulder,
Claudia winks to me
and marches toward
the bouncer guarding
the VIP area.

Claudia Bain

The Act

When you pretend
to be someone else for so long,
it becomes natural to not be you.

I straighten my posture,
shift gears in my mind from
Claudia Bain to
Claudia Bain SocialNet star,
Hollywood celebutante.

The Claudia who buys VIP access,
or screams until she gets what she wants.

The Claudia boys love,
men grovel for,
girls like Quinn flock to
for a moment of being seen.

The VIP bouncer stiffens seeing me approach;
he swallows hard, fortifying himself for
what's about to happen.

He knows his job,
and he knows he can't say no
to this Claudia.

This Claudia is the one people want.

Not the Claudia in the gym,
not the Claudia training with Master Oni,
not the Claudia who just wants a
warm hoodie and sweatpants.

"Is that the VIP area?"
I croon to him
swaying my hips in the serpentine flow
that draws his mind away from my face.

                    "Yes ma'am."
                    He looks for the bartender,
                    keeping his eyes away from me.

"Is there a cost to get in?"
I smile.

                    "In-n-nvitation-n only?"
                    he stutters.

Beatrix is further back,
watching this act.
What is she thinking?

"Can I get a pic with you
and the VIP area?"

Stretching my arm out
positioning the phone
I slip my other arm
around his shoulders
and draw close to his ear.
"Smile."

CLICK.

Beatrix smiles
seeing the bouncer's resolve dissolve.

        "Really Jimmy?"
        The bartender comes to us.
        "You going to break that easy?"

Beatrix laughs,
smiling, and comes up to
the bartender, bouncer, and me.

        "Y'all want to go that bad?"
        the bartender says.
        He looks to Beatrix.
        "You put her up to this?"

        Beatrix shakes her head,
        shrugs, and smirks.
        "It looked like a good book."

        The bartender bristles at that.
        "No. I don't think it is
        good.
        But, I don't like
        him being down there
        by himself with it."

The bartender motions for Jimmy to open the rope.

I put Claudia Bain SocialNet star
back in her closet.
Letting out the real Claudia Bain.
Sometimes I'm not sure which is which
but this one, the one coming out now,
is the one I like to see
in the mirror.

"Thanks Jimmy."
I punch his shoulder,
knocking him back from the door.

Beatrix Clark

The Invitation

Mike shivers
as we walk downstairs.
The chill catches me next
then ripples through Claudia.

"VIP area or ice box?"
I chuckle.

Mike doesn't laugh.
He forces a breath out
seeing the ice crystals
cling to the air around his mouth.

"HVAC issue?"
Mike says.

Claudia shivers.
"Are you sure about that?
This is more like
leaving a window open
in winter."

The upstairs was warm,
but maybe the AC is
blasting
up there to keep it cool
and the emptiness down here
makes it freezing?

That's it.

Red curtains hang over the last stair
and as Mike parts them
we walk through
to a 1930s speakeasy.

A few pool tables spot the floor
mixed with red velvet furniture
and dim Edison lights throwing an
orange glow over the room.

The walls are black bricks
making the size of the room
hard to determine.
A hallway opens in the back to
black walls lined with
bright colored doors.

"This is awesome."
Claudia gasps.
"VIP all the way."

Mike nods.
A proud smile grows.
"Yeah, I had to remodel
all this when I bought the place.

Use to be a bank.
I had some financial fortune
and made it what I wanted."

"The book?"

Mike pours himself a drink
and motions to us.
I shake my head;
Claudia does the same.

"Do you all know Russ?
Uh..."
Mike taps his head.
"Dr. Carlton?"

We nod.

"Yeah, he's the other member
of mine and Greg's trio.
Russ, Greg, and I grew up together
here in Richardsport.

I was never the academic type
but those two..."
Mike holds in a belly laugh.
"...they wanted to learn everything.

Russ was about..."
Mike flicks his fingers in quotes
"...science."
His quotes drop into
rubbing hands warming his fingers.
"And Greg was about philosophy."

"Why air quote 'science'?"
I interrupt.

Mike sighs,
this one weighed
with regret.

"Russ, well,
he means well.
Just he thinks there's
more to science than
empirical stuff."
Mike looks to the shining floor.
My eyes follow,
showing me the blurred reflection
of everything in the room.

"He was a doctor.

A medical doctor.
But something happened
at the university,
so now he just teaches.

No more research
or labs
or operations for him."

We sit with that last statement
hanging between us all
for a few minutes.

I look to Claudia,
all hints of fun chased away
with the sobering news
that one of our professors
or maybe even both
are crazy.

Drawing in a deep breath,
Mike starts again.

"Well, Greg and Russ
were kind of both outcasts
after Greg did that show."
Mike shakes his head.

"Alien Astronauts?"
I ask.
Claudia snickers
but I wave it off.
It was a good episode.

                    "Yeah, Greg's peers
                    said what he was
                    doing on that show
                    wasn't real research.
                    Just speculation and imagination
                    for a few quick bucks.

                    But I'll tell you,
                    he did that show for free.
                    He believed what he was saying
                    so much, he just
                    wanted to get the word out."

                    "I didn't see that episode..."
                    Claudia rolls her eyes,
                    dismissive.

"Dr. Roderick was talking about
his work on an ancient civilization
that could travel to other worlds."
Thinking about the episode,
the memory bubbles up.
"He said the lost society
kept very detailed books about
the technology that let them
travel the world but the books
were lost in some cataclysmic event.

There wasn't any historical record
of the event or the society
he was talking about.
Just some oral stories
passed down by generations."

Realization connects the dots
as I remember him pulling that book
into him like he was protecting it.
"Is that book one of those books?
One of the books that was supposed
to have been lost?"

Come.

I jump at the voice;
everyone follows
like moles
popping from their holes
waiting to be whacked.

"Did you hear something?"
Claudia whispers.

I nod.

We listen
acutely noticing
the colorful hallway
is empty

and silent.

"Probably one of the guests."
Mike watches the hall.
"I saw Greg come down
and..."
His eyes stay focused on the hall
but his thoughts trace the night,
trying to remember who else.

"Anyway..."
He returns to us
eyes jutting back
to the hall occasionally.
"...those two, Greg and Russ,
have been going deeper
into their studies
since then.

They figured no one believed them
so why not prove everyone wrong?"

Claudia gets up
her eyes cautiously pacing
from Mike to the hallway.

She paces like a cat
watching for a mouse
to come out of the hallway.

Her mind is on high alert,
repeating one word continuously:
breathe.

She's thinking about
martial arts classes with
someone.

A shiver of frozen air
rips through us all.

"But I've never seen them
like they were tonight."
Mike rubs his eyes;
a shiver sprints down his back,
mine as well.

That one wasn't from the cold.

"Russ left a note for Greg
earlier today.

Russ came in looking like..."
Mike shakes his head
searching for the words
to describe it.
"I mean...he wasn't himself.
Russ has always been
moody and dark but tonight
he was just empty.

He handed me that note
and there wasn't anything
in his eyes but focus
and intent.

He gave me
a note for Greg
and left.

Told me he had to 'get back,'
wherever that was."

Mike shivers.
"And when Greg
got here earlier,
he got that note
and hit the door faster
than a man chasing
his own ghost."

The leather binding
the aged pages
bubbles to my mind
as a blast of cold
gushes up from the hallway.

Was there a word
on the wind?

A whisper?

I look.

Claudia and Mike
look too.

Silence sits on us
pushing any breath we have
out
into the
choking
icy
air.

We wait.

Claudia's eyes say everything:
What was that?
Was that real?
Who's there?

Mike's the same.

But I know
what,
who.

The book.

It's whispering to us.

The White Room

Finally.

I drop the book
on my wooden desk
with a leaden slam.

No bounce.
No rattle
as the book
hits the wood.

Just dead
slam.

Then stillness.

Thick
stillness.

I pull my chair
across the concrete floor but
the rattling stutter of wood
doesn't break the stillness,
only scratches at it.

I sit
exhaling the breath
that has been waiting for this moment.

This book is it.
The instruction manual on
moving through the world with portals
and forgotten magics.

Magics to them back then,
technology to us today.
Would a search engine today
have been an Oracle to them back then?

Legends of this book say it was destroyed
in the mythical Library of Clmal,
like the Library of Alexandria but
with knowledge that was more
dangerous,
more
mystical.

It was
destroyed by
what the myths call
the Veil.

Probably a war
on the educated
where socialites
and athletes
were more celebrated than
academics.

Where your number of followers
mattered more than the
originality of your ideas.

Things don't change
all that much,
I guess.

Pulling back the cover
the spine
cries out -
no...that's not right -
the spine *chuckles*
as I open the cover.

The first page
stamped in aged black ink:

The Garden and the Well
by Lord Mot of Ugarit

Lord Mot, the
Library of Clmal Scribe
who traveled the world.

Scrawled below the title
scars of pen work
written in haste and madness.

   Greg, it's been looking for you too.
   -R

I smile.

My fingers slide over the page
crackling the paper
as I pull it over.

PART I: The Well

And I read
flipping each page
with racing eagerness.

Every flip unfolding a new revelation.

Every chapter twisting
the kaleidoscope of my universe.

Until the words stop becoming words.
They stretch to dark expanses
into which I jettison at light speed
with the lies of this world plucked from my eyes
and truths poured in to fill my mind.

Racing through space
through time
a screeching sound trails behind me
but I can't look back
too much to see in front of me.

I can't blink
I can't look away
I can only turn pages
as the words blaze through my mind
and the cold air of this world
burns my face

Until I look up
and see

PART II: The Garden

Around me
in the White Room
outlines of shadow
shift amongst the corners
stalking around the edges
of my sight.

One shadow comes over my shoulder
licking my ear
as it whispers,

*Yes. Show her.
Show her this
truth.*

Another shadow slithers up
from under my arm.
Its breath crystalizing on my chin.

*Go back.
Go to the Snow Library.
This can't be true.
Something's wrong.
Go back.
Take her with you.*

My fingers trace the drawings
in the book
following the curves and swirls
that show the Garden.

Those aren't plants
or vines.
The Garden isn't one
for growing beauty
only food.

Food for...?

*Yes. Find out.
Come and find out
in the basement
of the Snow Library.*

110

Come and see.

The Well is in the basement.
You must see it.

Take her with you.

The Garden awaits.
Russ is there
waiting for you.
You'll grow in the Garden.

Take her with you.

You will grow in the Garden.

So will she.

So will all.

The shadows' tongues
intertwine as they embrace
around me.

Over me.

Slurping each other
in an empty sucking sound
as each tries to pull life
from the other.

How do I know that?

The book, of course.

The book
has shown me
the shadows.

Shadows isn't right...
they aren't shadows,
they're blotches of outer space
engulfed in smoke and haze.

The Lightless

Yes, that's fitting.
The Lightless,
not just shadow but the
nonexistence of light.

At their center,
a spiral galaxy coils,
growling low as it turns
in the nothing of space.

The book
has shown me
the Garden
the Well
and now

I must see them
for myself.

Flying through the book
I stop
in space.

The complete absence
of heat
and light
doesn't hurt.

It should.

It envelops me
as if an inverse blanket
that leaves you cold and exposed.

An eye
turns to me
in that dark.

A black hole wobbling
amused laughter
as I fly away from it
seeing the stars and planets
orbiting it.

Flying farther away
to see the spiral galaxy
wreathed around the black hole
in white light.

It winks at me.

A word comes from that eye.
It loops in my mind...

Come.

I know the thing in the dark.

I know it
now.

My eyes return to the book,
to the streams of words pouring
into my conscious like molten brilliance.
Sprouts of understanding
root in the canyons of my mind.

I see.

Beatrix Clark

What is that?

Mike walks toward the hallway
listening closely.

Claudia strides forward
taking the lead while
shivering from the cocktail
of cold and adrenaline.

Her spine locks straight,
her knuckles popping
as fists coil tight.
Images flash in her mind
of people jumping out of the hallway
bursting out from doors
and the flurry of motions
she uses to handle
every situation.

She visualizes all the attacks
that could happen;
how she'd neutralize them
with brutal immediacy.

Shouldn't she be scared?
Fear drips from Mike's mind
but Claudia is steel.

Her breath frosts around her
as I look into the dark hallway.

The light is out.

The colorful doors
are dark.

Squeezing my chest with my arms
rubbing them over my jacket
I try to find warmth.

Looking back to the red curtains;
they don't sway.

Mike listens.

Claudia listens
knotting her black hair
into a tight coil.

I sift through the sounds
of chattering teeth
and shivering gasps
to hear anything.

Whispering.

"Do you hear that?"
The words fumble through
clattering teeth.

Mike and Claudia
shake their head.
Stilling themselves
to listen closer
to push their senses through the dark
but it is a wall.

A wall?

A door?

I step to the hallway;
Claudia pulls me back.

> "Are you crazy?"
> she whimpers.
> "Wait...are you..."
> She juggles the words
> looking for the right ones.
> "...getting something
> from the hallway?"

She waves her fingers
around her head.

"Not quite."
I shrug.
"Not sure, maybe just a feeling."

She nods
and moves out of the way
keeping close behind me.

Mike snaps around at that.
Facing us
I see his bluing lips.
He raises cupped hands to his mouth
and huffs hot air into them,
steam blowing out the small hole.

      "There isn't a broken HVAC unit,
      is there?"
      Mike mumbles.

I shake my head
through shivers and shakes.

"Where's the book?
I mean, which door
is Dr. Roderick's door?"

      "Greg's the..."
      A shiver quakes over Mike
      like a dog shaking off the rain.
      "Greg's the white door."

He presses into the cold
into the darkness
clawing a lighter from his pocket.

His thumb twitches uncontrollably
unable to line up with the igniter.
Crumpling forehead,
eyes turning to slits as he focuses
all energy on his thumb
to clip the wheel and press the tab
to make fire.

CLICK

CLICK

Mike shakes hard
trying to push out the shivers.

CLICK

Fire leaps out
and we instantly huddle around it
pulling in the miniscule heat,
but in this oppressive cold
it is enough to start our thaw
and light the way.

The blue door is first.

Then the green door.

>   "Russ's door."
>   Mike motions to the green door.

A white door is next.
It sweats with condensation.
Drips drool down the door
pooling on the shimmering hallway floor.

I look to Claudia -
she's pressed against me
letting me lead but ready to spring forward.
I'm not sure if she's shivering
or shaking with anticipation.

                              She looks to me
                              and ice crystals hang
                              from her eyelashes.
                              Picking up anything?
                              She pushes her thoughts to me.

I shake my head.

Mike reaches for the doorknob
snapping away as he touches it,
hissing.

                              "Burns,"
                              he whispers
                              through clattering teeth.

"Hot?"
I ask.

                              He shakes his head,
                              disbelief mixed with denial.
                              "Cold.
                              So cold...
                              it burns."

He stares at the doorknob,
blinking hard to see if it's real.
Can something,
something as mundane as a doorknob,
be so cold that it burns?

He bunches his shirt
around his hand
and reaches again for the knob.

Clenching it,
the ice crackles
and pings against the floor
as it falls.

Twisting the knob
Mike bursts into the room.

The White Room

Warmth blasts back against Mike
rushing over us in a choking desert wind.
Claudia springs around me
toward the door
as I spin to shield my face
from the burning
heat exploding from
the White Room.

Glancing in,
the name is fitting.
White bookshelves
line the white walls
circling a white floor
with a white carpet.

The only thing not white
in the room is
Dr. Roderick's clothes.
His face matches the décor.

Mike rushes to Dr. Roderick
sitting at his desk.
His arms rest beside the book
as the ancient pages flip themselves,
fanning his hair
billowing the frozen air
that was leaking out to us
in the VIP lobby.

Ice crystals dangle
from the bubbling drool leaking
from his lips
as his frost-crusted eyes
stare fixed into the book.

Mike rushes to him.
Shaking him.

Claudia reaches for me,
wet drips on her face.
Tears?

Remnants of ice crystals?

The walls inside the White Room
are sweating from the hot wind
swirling inside.

I reach for the air
to understand the cold
and the hot.
Kneeling down, I feel the dry heat
drifting up to us in serpentine waves
visible as a fog condenses
around our ankles.

Reaching up, the cold stings my fingers
as the higher I push my hand
the colder the air gets.

Wait, isn't that backwards?
Heat rises...

Claudia pulls me into her
with corded muscles tightening
under her tan skin.
She pushes into
the White Room.

Mike shakes Dr. Roderick.
Shouting to him.
"Greg! Greg!
Can you hear me!?
Greg!"

My eyes drop to the book.
The pages slow,
flipping,

flipping,

slowing

stopping on
a thick black ink drawing
of a building built into
a mountain.

There's something in the building
something I can see
if I stare harder.

Come.

I shiver again.
A convulsing tremor
seizing from my knees
to my neck
weakening every joint in between.

Claudia catches me
as I stumble.
"It's not over?"
She intertwines her long fingers
with my stubby ones.
"You're still cold, aren't you?"

I nod
as my hand escapes hers
and I step to the book.

Come...come...Beatrix...come...
Come to the library.
Let me in.

Golden pages
leather cover scent
I reach for it.

You could have saved him.
You warned him but he
didn't listen.

I can help you
discover your true power.

Just come to me.
Just let me in.
Come.

My fingers stretch to the book,
something drags me back.
A heavy weight pulls at me
dragging me away from the book
ripping at my jacket
with long strong claws.

Shouting behind me fades
as the book welcomes me into it.

Come.
Let me in.
I'll help you.
I'm at the library.

Mike's shouting fades.

All sound quiets in the drone of
static warbling
bubbling around me.

Resonating plucking in the static,
like a harp string strummed
clear and crisp,
comes from the book.

A music note.

High pitch reverberating
in a lovely invitation

to touch it

to pluck the string

the first notes
of a song.

My song?

I see the music,
the vibrating strings
growing out of the book.

Reaching for those golden strings
stretching up from the page
from the building in the mountain.

They were always there
but now I can see them,
I can feel their vibrations
calling for me to pluck them.

My hand is pulled back
the anchor dragging me away
from the book locking into place.

I must reach it.

Straining
I scream to feel the vibrations
their tingling touch just beyond my fingertips...

The room tilts
the walls falling up away from me
my back and head bouncing
off the floor
as I reach for those strings,
that pristine music.

I want it!
I need to feel it
that trembling vibration
tickling through my bones.

Closing my eyes
the book's song
goes distant
replaced by shouting.
Someone shouting in my face.

            "Beatrix!"
            Claudia's holding me
            on the floor.

Straddling me.
Blood dripping
from her mouth,
white knuckles
clenching my wrists.

Where's the book?

I look around
and see a red couch.
We're not in the White Room.

We're in the VIP room
where Mike told us about Dr. Roderick.
The plush red couch beside us,
black brick walls surrounding us.
How'd I get here?

Where's Mike and Dr. Roderick?

Where's the book?

A splash hits my cheek
snapping me back to Claudia's face.

She's bleeding.

Where's the book?

Where's my song?

"What..."
I shiver again.
"Where?"

The cold latches on to my bones
digging deeper like cavities
tickling my nerves.

"Are you back!?"
Claudia looks into my eyes.
Springs to her feet.
Grabs my jacket.
"We've got to go!

Something's coming!"
She rips me off the ground
up to my feet in a single
smooth lift.

"Mike? Doctor..."

"No! They're gone.
It's a...
shit, I don't know."

In her mind I see tendrils of
shadow and smoke crawling out of
the White Room floor.

She's processing her thoughts
making sense of what she saw
strands of darkness erupting
out of the book
twisting into fingers
made of inky drawings
twisting into an arm

reaching for
me...

The fire alarm snaps me out
of Claudia's mind
startling me to
see her face,
her panting
gasping breath.

Black fingers crawl out from
the White Room
slowly tapping toward us
in rippling puffs of smoke
and dust.

"GO!"
Claudia screams.

She drags me up the stairs
to an empty bar,
an empty dance floor.

Where'd everyone go?
How long was I out?

My legs fumble,
still weak.

My balance is broken
by the metallic clanging
of the fire alarm.
I clumsily match
Claudia's long stride
with my stubby legs.

"Get her out of here!"
Mike barks from behind the bar.
He cocks a shotgun and
runs toward the VIP stairs.

We cross the dance floor.
My legs go numb,
an arctic blast erupts from the VIP area
clinging to my ankle
ripping me back.

I fall.

Claudia pulls hard.
I look down to my heel;
black smoke tangles around my ankle.

Not smoke,
but black charcoal
lines jittering
and trembling
alive and solidifying
reaching for me
up the stairs that led to
the VIP room.

Fingers?

Claws?

The form comes into reality
as if being drawn to existence
with a thick black charcoal stump.

Ash and dust fall from the fingers
smearing and smudging across the floor
closing in on me.

But where is the rest of it?
This is just serpentine fingers
meeting in a curved palm
stretching from a pillar of
shadow and dust.

The pillar reaches down the stairs
impossibly long
as more smoke billows
from the VIP area
mounting
climbing
to black out
the stage lights
in a wall of black dust.

Claudia pulls on me.

BAM!

A siren goes off in my head
muffling Claudia's screaming
and Mike's shouting for us.

I'm snapped up by Claudia.
She rips me up
by my arm
tearing my jacket
keeping her fingers locked
on me.
She screams something in my face
then points to the door.

Mike runs toward the living charcoal drawing,
the mountain of dust building
behind us.

Claudia pushes me out the front door.
The night air dissolves the
muffled ringing in my ears
letting in the terror and rage
spilling out from the Vault.

Tripping down the stairs,
Claudia and I land on the sidewalk outside.
The door slams behind us.

The street is empty.

The line that wrapped around the building
now gone.

I turn to the Vault
seeing the oak door,
the iron banding,
shut.

Mike's in there.

Claudia runs to me,
grabs my shoulder.

"Are you...you?"

She looks deep into me.

"Who else would I be?"
I look to the door
waiting for Mike to come out
or to hear another shotgun blast.

Nothing.

Another shiver.

"The book had you,"
she says.
"It almost took you."

"Where's the book?"
I grab her shoulders
and look around her.

She pushes me away,
revulsion in her eyes.

"Mike's still in there!"

Dr. Roderick's thoughts
start coming to me.

Can't be true.
Gotta check the library basement.
Gotta see it for myself.

He's thinking about a well
in the basement of a library.

The library
where he found the book.
His mental map starts
to appear in my mind.

Claudia rushes to the door;
yanks it, rattles it.

The door doesn't open.

"Claudia."
I follow the map.
"There's something..."

"Help me!"
She keeps pulling on the door.
"Mike's in there!"

The book
calls me

whispering

Come.

Just let me in.
I have the answers.
Come. Let me in.

Beckoning me.

Begging me.

Come.

Demanding.

And so
I follow.

Chapter 3

Kindling (10 years ago, today)

"Don't go Dad!"

I beg him to stay.
Something's going to happen
on this trip.

It's bad.

Dad smiles.
"I have to go, but
before I do, I have
something for you."

He pulls out
a little box from his pocket.
It's pretty.
Has a pretty woman on it.

She looks like me.

"This will help you
find your way
if you ever get lost."
I open the box.

Cards are in the box.
Gray cards
with gold lines on them.
Pictures are on the other side
of the cards.

"I don't want cards.
I want you to stay."
I grab his waist
squeezing him to stay
dropping the cards
spilling on the floor.

Mom's going to be mad
about the mess
but I need him to stay.

I need him to listen.

"Don't go! Don't fly!"
I scream so he hears me.

"Beatrix Clark,
get a hold of yourself!"
Mom peels me
from Dad
and kisses him goodbye.

"Mindy will be over later,"
Dad says.
"And you'll forget
all about me."
He smiles and laughs.
"You two will be reading
until I get back
I bet."

"Dad, something's going to happen.
The flight, something-"

"Don't talk like that
Beatrix!"
Mom squeezes my arm,
shakes me to shake away
the thoughts.

"I have a feeling-"

"Feelings don't stop
the world from happening."
Dad smiles
through a sadness
growing on his face.

"I've got to go.

And you've got to stay here
and help your mom."
Dad nods to Mom.

Nothing I say
will stop him.
What's the use of knowing
what's going to happen
when I can't do anything about it?

But I don't know
what's going to happen.

I just have a feeling.

And it's bad.

Dad kisses my cheek
and gets in his car.
He waves as he backs out
of the driveway.

And then
a trash truck slams into him.

Mom screams
seeing the explosion of
glass
steel
plastic.

Dad's head explodes on the driver side window
as the truck rips the car in half
sending the back half tumbling
into the neighbor's bay window.

I scream.

I can't cry.
The feeling
that this
could have been
avoided
devours all the emotions
that should be growing inside me.

If only he believed me.
If only he knew my feelings
weren't just feelings.

Mom runs to the car's remains,
to the splattered thing
that was Dad.
The neighbor's house
is on fire.

Another neighbor
tackles Mom down
as she claws
and flails
and begs,

"No! No!"

I think about the timing,
the good luck Dad thought he'd had
with an earlier flight.

I had a feeling about this timing.

I've been having a lot of feelings lately
and they've all been bad.

Why didn't he listen?
I look at the cards he gave me
and wonder if
he would have listened
to them?

Dr. Gregory Roderick

Ghosts and Lies (A few moments ago…)

"Greg! Greg!
Can you hear me!?
Greg!"

Mike shakes me.

The shadows are gone.
They drank each other
into nothingness
leaving me with the quiet
and the book
and Mike

and Beatrix
and her friend?

"What's going on?"
I grab Mike,
pushing him back.

Beatrix reaches for the book;
her friend is trying to pull her back.

But she can't have Beatrix.

The book wants her.
And Beatrix wants the book.

But...I'm not finished.
This isn't just a book.
There's something more here.
The shadows said the answers
are in the Snow Library basement.

What is in the basement of
the library?
A well?

I pull the book to me;
it jumps away
toward Beatrix.

Slamming it shut

Beatrix's blank face
snaps to wrath
her eyes boiling with hatred
her teeth bare.

I jump from my chair
the book clattering to the floor
flipping open.

Beatrix snarls and pounces toward it.
Her friend clutches her
ripping her away.

Beatrix screeches
a banshee scream.
Denied her soul's desire.
She rounds on her friend
hammering the girl in the face
knocking her back on her heels.

Blood bursts from the girl's lips
spraying in arcs over the White Room
landing on the book's open page.

Frozen air
bursts from the page
knocking me back.

Beatrix's frenzied rage
struggles against Mike and the girl
knocking Beatrix over,
carrying her out the White Room.

I snatch up the book
as the blood slides off the page
hitting the floor.

Strands of black ink
swirl in the blood
charcoal branches exploding from the drop
latching on to the floor
clawing in convulsing grasps
seizing out of the droplet.

A gurgling chuckle comes from the
growing ink pool
as black veins
struggle along the carpet
toward the door.

Chuckling
grows to gasping laughter
as a web of veins approaches
the door
reaching out the White Room.

Reaching for her?

The library.
I need to get back.
See the basement.
The Well?

Running from the White Room
passing Beatrix being restrained
by the girl and Mike
near the red VIP couch.

I don't stop,
bursting up
the VIP stairs.

My shoulder gets ripped back.
Mike stands there.

                        "What the hell man!?"
                        he screams over the music.

"I've gotta get back
to the library!"
I point
beyond the door
to the water taxi.

Beatrix screams
from being restrained;
her pleads
and growls
and hisses
are clear.

They ring over the music.
Heads start turning,
dancing and thrashing bodies stop
looking at Mike and me.

Mike snaps back to the VIP area
as the new bouncer starts down.

> "Jimmy! NO!"
> Mike looks around.
> "Get everyone out of here."
> He pushes Jimmy
> toward the onlookers,
> shouting over the music
> and Beatrix's screams.
> "Get them out!"

Panic flooding Mike.
He runs to the fire alarm
rips it down
pulling the plug on the music
starting the metal-on-metal clanging
that shuts down your brain
only letting one thought
remain:
Run.

Everyone does.

They sprint for the doors
tripping over each other
with the chaotic abandon
that drives all exodus.

I follow
grabbed again by Mike.

"What did you do!?"
he screams over the
fire alarm's clanging
that echoes through me.

"I was right!"
I shake the book.

Laughter bubbles up from the VIP area.

It isn't the girls laughing.

It's the thing,
the thing growing from the
blood and ink.

Mike hears it.

He runs to the bar.

I run out the door
passing Danny
telling him,
"Run!
Everyone's out!"

The water taxi is ready
to go back
to the library.

Jumping in.

I go.

Returning (Now)

I look down Curson Street
from Ross Street.

One light
can be seen at the end.

The flickering orange light
of the library.

I go to the light.

Ascending the stairs
of the library,
the door is open.
I step into the darkness
and leave the door as I found it.

If the thugs come again,
so be it.
My need for answers
outweighs the need for survival.

Curiosity
has overridden
common sense.

Frigid air wafts up
from the basement.
The smell is the same
as the air from the book,
the frost on my cheeks
from the VIP area.

No lights.

On the checkout counter,
I find a flashlight
and it works.

I didn't expect it to.

Flashlights always fail
in horror movies.

But
I'm not in a horror movie.
I'm living my life.
I'm finding my research
and the shadows said the basement
was the answer.

Pushing the basement door open
the creaking hinges
yawn in the boredom
of inevitability.

They knew I'd be back
but perhaps
didn't expect me
to be alone.

Why didn't I bring Beatrix?
It wanted me to.

The book invited her.

I should have
brought her, but
what would I say?
'Hey student, come with me.
I'm breaking and entering.'

I don't think tenure
would protect me
in that scenario.

Going downstairs,
each wooden stair
strains to hold splinters together
as I step down
down
down
to the concrete floor.

Last time I was here,
I went upstairs to find the book;
now I'm going downstairs to find
more answers.

My flashlight catches
a work bench full of rusty tools
a bookshelf strewn with camping gear
a stone well with a thick wooden cover.

Lingering on the well
I remember the entry from the book:
PART I: THE WELL.

The wooden cover is so thick
it looks
immovable.
Iron banding loops and swirls
over the wood in symbols familiar
from the book.

Letting my light wander,
I look to the tools.
Woodworking tools?
Saws, orange crust dulling the steel.
Chisels, chipped and ground down from work.
Nails, twisted out of something.

Clattering rattles through the room.

Instinct snaps my eyes
to the well.

Was that clatter
wood on stone?
Was it real
or the product of
strange tales from the book
and rusty tools on the table?

Quiet seeps into the basement again.

The flashlight crawls over surfaces
throwing long slithering shadows
between the storage shelves.

Are those just shadows
or snakes wiggling away from the light?

My anxiety unfurls
sending shivers through my body
ending in a whiplash to the flashlight.

The wooden lid
is on the well.

It's thick.

Looks heavy
like a wooden coin
sealing the well.

I wait.

For what?

For the clatter again.
For the lid to explode off
and the horrors from the book
to slither forth and engulf me.

The lid
is still.

The air
seems thin
harder to breathe
my chest tightens.

Scanning with the flashlight
finding the bookshelf again.

Camping gear
mounds up on the shelves.
Fuzzy coats hang beside the shelves
with brown fur sticking out
from the hooded parkas.

Gas lanterns,
bags of mushy camp meals,
blocks of coffee.

Clatter.

Sweeping back to the lid,
to the wood on stone clatter,
to where I know the sound was.

The lid
is still.

A whine presses through
my throat
like a thin whistle
like a teapot about to scream.

I want to call out
I want to say,
"Who's there?"
authoritative and dire.

But I only have
a thin whistling whine
and shaking hands
making the flashlight convulse.

Shadows dance
in a frenzy now
and nothing is still

except

the lid.

Walking to the well,
I press on the lid
feeling its immensity,
the weight of ancient trees
sealing whatever is
inside.

Recoiling from the lid
a splinter from the wood
stabs under my index fingernail.

The splinter
twists like the rusty nails on the table.
It peeks out from under my nail,
winking to me with a small tip.

Tucking the flashlight into my armpit
I grab at the splinter
but miss it.

Holding my hand in front of the flashlight
I pinch to pry it out but still miss.
Looking closer
the splinter wriggles
and slithers deeper
disappearing into the white flesh
under ridges and ripples
of my fingernail.

Clatter.

The flashlight drops
cracking on the floor
stealing the light from me.

I listen.
My ears push through
the pulsing heartbeat
heating my face
and drying my mouth.

Dropping to the floor
I feel for the flashlight
sliding my fingers over
cold smooth concrete.

My fingers hit something
hard metal rough
gripping the flashlight.
I grab it
and push the button.

Click.

No light.

Banging it against my hand
rattling the batteries inside,
press again.

Click.

No light.

Cringing
pain in my finger
wracks my body
crumbling me.

Itching crawls
under my skin
down my finger
pain
straining
wrapping me up.

The splinter?

Yes, the splinter
entangles around my bones
weaving through muscles
holding me frozen.

Paralyzed.

Footsteps upstairs.

Someone is in the library.

"H-"
Pain stitching my throat shut
silencing my screams
leaving only tearing eyes
to plead for someone
anyone to help.

Silent shouting
is drowned in a slopping slushing noise
that squishes toward me.

The flashlight flickers on
lighting a fleshy bulge
dangling from the lip
of the well.

It spills to the floor
with a splat.
Bubbles of slime
pop and drool where it moves.

The worm stretches
as something inside it strains
to break free.

I'm petrified by the splinter.

It doesn't hurt anymore
but I can't move,
trapped waiting
for the worm
wriggling
lurching
toward me.

The book falls from my jacket
clattering to the ground
leather cover slapping the concrete floor.

the book whispers in my mind.

It's smiling.

I know it is.

Happy to trap me.

Did it trap Russ?

Am I just the next victim?

"Hello?"
Beatrix says upstairs.
"Is anyone here?"
she calls out softly.
"Dr. Roderick?"

The worm's flesh bursts open
as teeth spill out
unfolding
thin
jagged
like nails
torn from wood.

I look up the stairs
and try to scream
to warn her
to run
but

nothing comes out.

The book
laughs.

Better off…

At the end of Curson Street
I see a flickering orange streetlight.

A library?

Is it a song?

A feeling?

A rippling vibration?

Something tells me
that's where the book is.
That's where Dr. Roderick went.

Whatever this energy is,
whatever sense it is engaging,
it pulls me to that light.

Stopping,
looking back
two men follow me
keeping their distance.

I try to read them
but can't.

They push me away,
walling me out.

A literal wall in their minds
like the brick walls I've been building
in my own mind.

My heart thumps
as they walk toward me.
I try to read them again
but I'm swept away
so fast I get dizzy.

Only the
library light
can see me in this alley.

I run to it.

Work boots
run after me.

The book whispers...

Come.

You'll be safe here.

Metal letters catch
the golden light
reading
Snow Library.

I run up the stairs to the entrance
and push through the door.
It's open.

My eyes adjust
too quickly to the dark
bringing all the forms of
the library out of the murky dark,
shadows drowning everything.

Scanning the entrance,
piles of books tower around me
I could hide in forever.

The boots are getting
closer.

I look back
to see the men
hoping to see
Claudia or anyone else
running behind them.

I shouldn't have come here
alone.

> *You're not alone,*
> the book croons.

I'm downstairs.

The book?

I check again for
Claudia and see
a flashlight
at the end of the street.

Could be her,
but I can't wait.
She'd probably run.

Don't run.
Join me in the basement.
I have so much to show you.

I can show you the real you,
the powerful you that
your father
would have listened to.

And I have a way out.
Come to me.
Come.

I creak down the wooden stairs
and into the darkness.

Descending into that lightless
cavern of a basement,

my eyes readjust...

Slipping,
catching the railing,
my legs shoot out
from under me.

Crashing down
on the concrete floor
my hand slaps a splashing
thick slime on the floor.

Holding up my hand,
the darkness can't hide the
smell and shine of
a thick blood slick
dripping down my forearm.

My jeans soak it up,
drinking in the slick pool
around me.

I crawl out of the pool
following the streak of blood
to a stone well in the center
of the room.

The book is angled against the well.

Hello.
It sighs.

I pick it up
running my hand over
the smooth leather
feeling the rippling vibrations
creeping from my fingertips
to my spine.

Inhaling the smell of
musty paper
but the scent is tainted
by the sharp copper
of blood that fills
the basement.

There's a messenger bag on the bookshelf
with camping supplies.
I grab the bag and shove the book in.

Easier to carry.

Someone stops
at the top of the stairs.
Their shadow is thrown
long and dark
down the stairs
by a flashlight's glow.

I squeeze the book
into my chest.

Turning,
feeling the
rough bricks,
crumbling grout.

I grab the edge
pulling a brick loose.

It hits the concrete floor
with a shattering crash.

The shadow at the stairs
stops and opens the door wider.
A work boot hits the stair
sending a groan through the basement
as the owner steps on it.

Now. You have to go now,
the book pleads.

*Go, now!
It isn't deep.*

I grab the ledge
and climb over.

CRACK!

A shadowy body tumbles
downstairs bouncing
breaking, snapping
the wooden stairs.

Looking down
the well looks deep,
but the book
keeps telling me
it's not.

I climb down
to hide.
Letting my fingers hold onto the ledge,
lowering myself into the well,
the grout crumbles,
the brick I'm holding slips
and I fall into a blast of cold
as the well vanishes
into darkness
and then
I'm not falling.

I'm standing
on a black beach
underneath a roaring
green nebula.

Where did the well go?

My world...
it's gone.

Claudia Bain

Pursuit (a few moments ago…)

"Mike!"

I pull on the door
but it won't open.

"Help me Beatrix!"

Banging on the door,
screams come from the other side
but not
human
screams.

A shotgun blast
erupts.
A squeal follows.

"Beatrix!"

I turn.

She's gone.

She runs up the street
probably after the book.
Going to her book.
Needing her book.

She's running,
showing the energy she had
when she was fighting me
in the Vault.

I haven't seen someone
go from calm, nice person
to feral monster
since the last time
I took away Jasmine's heroin.

WHAM!

White stars pop around fading black
as I fall down the stairs.
Vision goes fuzzy.

BAM!

Another shotgun blast.
This one closer.

SLAM!
Giant wooden doors
clatter and **cha-chunk** close.

I roll down the stairs
hearing the hard panting
of someone chasing me.

> "Run!"
> Mike shouts
> scooping me up.

I stagger to my feet
shaking away the stars
from the door smashing into me.

Kicking off my heels,
I don't wait,
I don't ask why.
I sprint
pulling Mike
toward Beatrix's path.

"What was that!?"

                              "Just run!"

Grabbing Mike's arm
I pull him upright
to a running position.

Most people have horrible running form.
Mike's most people.

"Stretch your legs!
Think gazelle, not
whatever you're doing!"

Pulling in the mental image
I stretch my legs
stretch my core,
breathe like Master Oni showed me,
making myself lighter.

Mike's carrying a flashlight
that flickers and flashes
around the streets
as he pumps his arms
running in his tense,
strained posture.

Good call.
Flashlight could be handy
but not as handy as that
shotgun.

An explosion of thick splinters
behind me signals that the doors to the Vault
have been ripped off.

I glance back.

Writhing shadowy smoke
pours out the Vault
into the night.

It screams and wails
as police sirens approach.

"Don't look!
Just run!"

      "Telling me or you?"
      Mike pants.
      "Where's Greg?"

We round the corner
watching Beatrix take the next
alleyway.

Each turn
she's just ahead at the next.
I point to her turning on
Curson Street.

We stop at the corner of Curson
seeing her go into an
old library.
The lights are out
except the flickering golden light
by the door.

Darkness waits for her inside.

Two men are chasing her
deeper into Curson Street,
right into the library,
right to the book.

Mike grabs his knees
gasping for breath.
I pull him forward.

"Beatrix needs help."

                              "You sure?"
                              He sucks in air
                              puffing it out.

He drinks air
like a drowning man
drinks water;
it will nourish him
the same.

Pointing to the men
going into the library
I grit my teeth
and nod,
taking a
centering breath.

"Yes!"
I start down Curson Street.

Mike pulls me back.
I round on him
ready to stomp him.

                              He puts his arms up in surrender
                              and backs off.
                              "Just sayin',
                              you saw what happened
                              in there.
                              She wanted the book.
                              And it wants her."

He thumbs back
as wisps of shadow
slither into the golden
streetlights.

                              "She punched you in the face!
                              She don't want help."

"They never do."
Beatrix makes sense now.
Addicts isolate.
Addicts fight.
Addicts lie and lose control.
Addicts run into dark places
with malicious people to get
their fix.

I guess you don't have to
numb yourself to the world
with drugs and alcohol
when you can escape
into books.

"I'm not leaving her."
Watching the shadow approaching.
"And I'm not waiting
for that thing to get here."

Mike sighs and coughs,
grabbing his side
as we run
to the library.

No point being stealthy,
I bust in and put my bare foot full force
through the first guy's spine
tumbling him downstairs.
Mike stomps the other guy in the sternum
sending him flying,
exploding the towers of books
in his flight path.

I follow the first guy
downstairs
seeing Beatrix's purple hair
dip into the well
and her fingers slip,
vanishing into the dark.

"Mike!"

I pull out my phone
and activate the flashlight to see.

Blood trails from the
base of the stairs
to the stone well
in the center of the room.

The guy I kicked down
is a crumpled mass
on the concrete floor.

He's breathing.

Barely.

"That thing's coming!"
Mike runs downstairs
slamming the door
behind him.

"Whoa!"
He stops at the blood
and crumpled body.
"Is he…?"

"Breathing?"
I confirm, feeling the heat
under his nose.
"Yeah…"

"Is this from Beatrix?"
Mike sucks in breaths
through the stitch in his side
stretching to find a
comfortable position.

Near the well is a shelf
with camping supplies.
I grab a flashlight
and flick it on.

Going to the well,
I look down
seeing just a black hole.

No bottom.

Cold drifts up just like
in the Vault VIP area.

"No. I don't think so. She just dropped
down this well but I don't see anything."

At the supply shelf,
I grab a coat, toss one to Mike.
Sizing the boots to my foot,
grabbing climbing gear,
ice axes,
rope,
clamps,
throwing it all
into a backpack.

Blankets,
food packs,
this place has everything.

I look to the Well
and wonder what's down there
with supplies like this
right beside it.

"Where'd she go?"

                      "Who?"
                      Mike says
                      looking back to the door.

He stays on the stairs
wringing his shotgun
and choking through
his exhausted breaths.

"Beatrix.
I saw her go down here."
Light sticks are on the
shelf with the camping gear.

Snapping one
I throw it down
the well.

It vanishes.

Not devoured by the dark,
just gone.

"Beatrix!"
I shout.

"Did you see Greg too?"
Mike pants.

"No. She probably followed him
down to get the book."
I look around -
no sign of the book
in the bloody streaks
and bubbling slime
on the floor.

The door rattles.
A snarling screech
comes from the other side.

"It's here."
Mike straightens up
his eyes flying to the door.
"The thing from my bar."

Mike holds up the gun.

Rappelling gear is on the shelf.

"Mike!
Down the well!"

A climbing bolt is in the wall.
Pulling on it,
it doesn't move.

I snap a line on it
and run to the well.

"Mike!"

I scan the room with my flashlight
finding another one on the floor
rolling on the concrete.
Picking it up,
pushing it into my backpack.

No doors.

No windows.

No way out
but the well?

I snap a line for Mike.
and climb onto the well wall.
"Come on!"

The door crunches
and cracks
as Mike steps over the body.
The crumpled man grabs his foot.
Mike falls.

                              "Ack!"
                              Mike turns and stomps
                              but the man climbs
                              his leg.

The door shatters down
as a shadowy arm
grabs the crumpled man
and rips him up the stairs
screaming.

Mike is free.
"Mike!"

I throw him the line.

He grabs it.

Pulls up to his feet
and jumps with me
down the well.

II

Who We Are
Who We Could Be
Who We Wish We Were

Chapter 4

Awakening

Black sand squishes
around my feet like wet asphalt.
I sink in slowly,
anchored by the
warm tingle
growing up
my legs.

Invisible energy
grows inside my veins
branches throughout my torso
climbs down my arms
around my throat
into my eyes
standing every hair
on end.

The stars
glow brighter
burning my eyes
with their pulsing
white light.

I feel...

Amazing.

I'm glowing...

> *You're charging,*
> *You're special, Beatrix.*

I watch in awe
as waves of pink light
drift off me like
heat from a car hood
on a winter morning.

> *You know electricity?*

I nod.

> *You're like a battery*
> *for this energy.*
> *That's why I brought you here.*
> *I knew you would be safe here*
> *because you are powerful here.*

"Where am I?"

The shattered blue planet
on the horizon and
the forest green nebula
sprawled in the starry sky above
tell me I'm not
in Richardsport anymore.

> *We will have time for that.*
> *In the forest...*

I look ahead of me
and see a charcoal black forest
at the end of a gray grass field
off the black sand beach.

> *...you will find a library*
> *with an artifact that will*
> *help you realize your true*
> *power.*
>
> *You'll need it here.*
>
> *This place is*
> *home to many...*
>
> *fiends.*

I nod
feeling the urgency
in the book's direction.

My feet move,
pushing me into
the black forest.

Living Forest

Do you see the path?

Its voice is clear
and louder here
than back in Richardsport.

I can hear it
like it is whispering
directly into my ear.

Hot breath and all.

"Yes."
The sand turns to
gray grass blades
crunching and crumbling
under my steps.

Grass turns to
small stones to
gravel.

Dust kicks up
with each step
shrouding my ankles
with a faint gray cloud.

Follow it,
the book whispers,
encouragement heavy
in its tone.

*It will take you to
the Library of Clmal.*

"What's at the library?"
Leaves and branches
stab into the path
snagging my jacket
and bloody jeans.

I look like I swam through blood
to get here.
My purple Docs are dark brown,
my jeans are splotched rusty red.

Is that blood from
Dr. Roderick?

What did that?

*Best not to dwell on that.
Focus here.*

*As I said, there are many
fiends in this place.
Focus on the library.*

*There you'll find an artifact
that will help
open a doorway home,*
the book answers
quietly.

Why would I want that?

This place is amazing
and I feel
strong.

A thicker jacket
would have been smart.
The cold of this place
feels the same as the cold
from the Vault.

A flashlight
would be handy too.
But my faint pink glow
is enough to see
where I'm going.

I slow
as a dust cloud
drifts from something
hunched over
in the center of the path.

Sloshing sounds
slobber from
the huddled thing.

I stop.

Look for a way around it.
None found.

Going through the trees
and branches
will make some sound...

A wet snort rattles out
of the thing
as something like a head
pops up from the body.

The leaves and branches
around me reflect my
radiating glow.

A pink glowing person
standing against a backdrop
of black leaves and charcoal branches.

No hiding here.

> *No need to hide.*
> The book chuckles
> in my mind.
>
> *Feel the energy of*
> *that creature.*
> *Pull from it,*
> *use it against it.*

No sooner had the book said it
than I start to feel warmth
from the thing
in the dust cloud.

Every tiny hair on my body
points to the
thing in the dust
as if it were a magnet
pulling me toward it.

Strands of light
stretch through the dust cloud
hanging and writhing like lightning
that can't discharge.

Constant
whips of light
reach toward
the lightning
growing from my fingers.

> *Yes, grab those*
> *wisps of light*
> *and pull with your mind*
> *not your arm,*
> the book says.

The shadowy creature turns
toward me in the dust cloud.
Five legs crack and pop
as it runs at me.

Snapping sounds make me
imagine crab claws
or spider mandibles
eager to tear into me.

Each leg's extension cracking
arthritic bangs
as it kicks up dust
into a cloud.

My strands of light wrap around
the thing with ease.
I close my fingers into a fist,
feeling the energy,
feeling the live wire,
and I visualize pulling
that energy into me.

It's natural.

Doesn't take deep thought
or hard concentration.

It just flows.

The dust cloud slows,
it dissipates,
leaving a crumbling
dark gray
five-legged scorpion snake creature
a few feet away from me.

It gasps a whine from
its cobra-shaped head
but that too is choked away
with me pulling its strands.

It's done.

Let go.

I should let go.

But I don't.
I pull in more
energy.
More of whatever this is.
Feeling the warm vibrations
claw through my hand
and into my body
stretching the warm
charging sensation
throughout my spine.

The creature's body
calcifies and crumbles
to something like the gravel
under my feet...

Dust floats up from it
and the energy runs dry.

All gone.

The lightning
fades from white
to blue
to gone.

I release the thread
that was never there.

"Did I just kill it?"
The dust cloud
drifting to the ground
answers for me.

I couldn't stop.
The energy just kept going
and I couldn't stop drinking it in.

And I killed it.

And worse of all,
it felt good.

And I'd do it again
even though I know I shouldn't;
the warmth in me surges
and begs for more.

I shouldn't
have liked it,

but I did.

I smile.

Memories on the Road

The forest isn't as dark.

The black and charcoal tones
of leaves and branches
now ripple with my
pink and purple glow.

I'm a power station.

This energy just wants to
explode
from within me.

Rustling of leaves
doesn't panic me
as I see those invisible threads
writhing from the creatures
lurking beyond where I can see.
I grab them.

The book was right.
I'm powerful here.

The bolts of lightning
flickering and swaying from
creatures that look like armored snakes
with curved tails and crab snappers -

scorpion snakes.

Their strands slide into my hand
and I take a long drag
like fresh coffee during an all-nighter.

Surging
pulsing
raging
energy.

The second one
that rushes me,
I turn to dust instantly.

It was going to attack me.
To it, I was just food.

I am a power station.

The rustling quiets
and I keep walking.
Dust coming up around me
as I light the darkness
of this place.

Another scorpion snake
jumps into the path
and rushes toward me.

My hands jut out
snatching the lightning
and turning the creature
to dust.

I don't feel anything
this time.
No remorse.
I'm just defending
and these things are attacking.

The scorpion snakes
mistake me as prey.

More scorpion snakes,
three this time,
swing down from the trees.

I push my hands out at them,
the lightning from my fingers
cutting through the creatures
like whips.

How did I know to do that?

A wolf isn't taught
how to bite.
The book laughs.

This place awakens the wolf
in you Beatrix.

I'm not a wolf.

I'm not as bright?
My pink-purple glow
has dimmed from floodlight
to flashlight.

You're a battery,
the book says
with dull disinterest.

Current, in this case,
the energy
you think,
is magic, flows in and out.

You absorb it,
you get brighter.

You expel it,
you dim.

But...
"Magic?"
This is real magic,
not just knowing things
or channeling through the cards.

I can't do magic...

How many times
could I have used this?

The book was right,
if I could have shown this to Dad
I could have stopped him from
going on that trip.

And if I had done that
what else would have changed?

Mom wouldn't have shut down.

Mindy wouldn't have had to move back home
to her horrible family.
She couldn't escape.
My family was her escape,
and with that gone,
she took the only way out left.

I could have saved all three of them
with just this little ability.

And then what?

Would I have
been alone
all those years?

Helping Mom make it through
every day,
reminding her to eat,
shower,
sleep.

Could I have been the child
and she be my mom?

My palms are wet.
Blood slips from the slits
my fingernails dig into my palms.
A song emerges from the
grinding of my teeth
and drips of blood hitting
the leaves at my feet.

A song of
all that could have been.

Dad wouldn't have died today.
Mindy wouldn't have killed herself
three weeks from today.
Mom wouldn't have lost her job,
her will to live.

I wouldn't have lost
everything.

A pack of those
scorpion snakes snap and hiss
further up the path.
They fight over something,
squabbling as their strands lash around.

That's what I need.
I grab at them,
ripping their lightning into my hands,
and smile as I get ready to feel
something else.

Something beyond the song of what could have been.
What should have been.
If I wasn't too stupid or weak
to see what I can do now.

Drinking them
I ignore the squeals of surprise
and confusion,
focusing on the
warm and freeing energy
trickling into me
dissolving the song
screaming in my mind
reminding me of what
should have been.

I close my eyes
to enjoy drowning
in the numbness.

Leaves and branches explode toward me
throwing splinters and sticks
as a massive body rushes from the forest.

A pyramid-shaped appendage
spears one of the scorpion snakes
and then spirals apart
unleashing a coil of fangs.
Fleshy jaws flex and stretch
wrapping around the scorpion snake
with a wet chomp, unleashing
a burst of blue sludge.

Rising up,
the pyramid reveals itself
as this new creature's head;
three arms, two legs
stretch to gather the other fleeing
scorpion snakes.

I release them
and reach for this new monster's energy.
But...its strands don't just float around;
they drift toward me
and snap away.

I grab at the threads
but can't get them.
Each is snapped away
just as I'm about to get it.

It's baiting me...

It turns to me.
Stretching its body
revealing thick muscle under
flabby flesh.

This creature looks like a satyr
with a millipede's segmented abdomen.
Its strands of lightning
snap and flick like fuzzy feelers
around its body.

The pyramid topping its body
trembles, releasing a
rumbling snarl.

Its upper body drops to the ground
and it charges
the body weaving
slithering
twisting each segment
as the three arms
working as six fingered claws
rip through the forest dust.

I put out my hands
but one of its wisps of lightning grabs me
lassoing my arm
coiling with my own strands.

The draining comes immediately
showing me what those other things
felt when I pulled from them.

Light rushes out of me
through the thread
as another string of lightning wraps my ankle
ripping more energy from me.

Pulling back away
I can't break free
feeling exhausted
weakening
growing
small.

My legs
buckle.

Dig deep!

You've got more in you!

Another strand
from the creature
wraps me in a noose
tightening
squeezing
life
out

BAM!

CHICK CHICK!

BAM!

Dust puffs up around me
as I hit the ground
feeling the lightning
release.

Darkness of the forest returns
sitting heavy on my chest
stomping out my breath.

I roll over
looking up
seeing the giant monster's rows of razor teeth
blasted off its pyramid head
by Mike's shotgun.

Claudia jumps over me
sinking an axe into the thing's knee
sending the creature sprawling to the ground.

She rips the axe loose
and buries it again
into the thing's chest
or what should be its chest.

Blue sludge erupts from the wound.

Mike blasts another shot
at the monster's head
and it stops twitching.

The lightning
vanishes as the shotgun blast
echoes through the forest.

"Beatrix!"
Claudia shouts
as she scoops me up.

She doesn't have strings?
"Can you hear me!?"

I look to Mike
seeing the wriggling white strands
flailing around him
and look again to Claudia
seeing
nothing.

Curious...?
the book says
with wonder.

"Yes,"
I answer them both.

Claudia Bain

About Time (a few moments ago...)

"Ah what the-"
Still holding the rope
I'm standing on a
black beach
under
a shattered planet.

Stars hang above
me and Mike
as we let go
of the ropes that
don't exist anymore.

A green glowstick sits in the sand
beside my foot.
The one I threw down the well?

"I was dropping,
now I'm here."

"Yeah, I'm all out
of dealin' with weird shit
tonight."
Mike shakes his head.

Waves crash on the sand
in rolling gray-white caps.
Silver shells
or rocks
tumble out of the waves.

Boney yellow boulders
stick out of the beach
like knuckles breaking through
soft skin.

There's no sign of the well,
or the rope,
or the-

"Mike, take cover!"
I point to the closest boulder,
run to it, and duck down.
Mike follows.

                              "What-"

"Shhh!"

From where we appeared
a pillar of black smoke
springs out of the ground
and pools in the air.

Whips and wisps of darkness
writhe and ripple
into a cloud
that rushes off into the forest
breaking away from Beatrix's footprints.

It vanishes into the
black forest.

"Let's find Beatrix and
get the hell out of here."
I point to the
footprints in the sand.

> "I'm here for Greg,
> not Beatrix.
> Sorry 'bout your friend
> but I've gotta look out
> for mine."
> Mike shakes his head
> his eyes following the footprints
> up the beach.

"Those are Beatrix's prints.
Too small for Dr. Roderick's
and shaped like boots, not
loafers."

I point to a streak in the sand.
"My guess is someone got dragged there."

> "What are you, Daniel Boone?"
> Mike whispers, snarky tones
> taking over his chill attitude.

"Wilderness survival skills.
Tracking is a fundamental thing
if you want to be able to eat."
Scanning the black tree line,
seeing nothing,
I stand and motion Mike to follow.

"We'll find Dr. Roderick. But I'm guessing
he's going to need more than you and me
if he's been dragged off.
Let's get Beatrix
and we'll come back
for him.
If we split up,
we're going to get picked off
by whatever's in there."

I nod to the forest.

Did a fire make the trees
black like that?
A poisoned world?
Is it dead?

Mike nods
pulling the shotgun from his belt.

"How many shells?"
I pull out two ice axes
from the backpack.

Never trusted any weapon that needs ammo
or any parts other than me
working it.

> "Two pockets full."
> He shoves his hand into his
> pocket and pulls out a shell.
> "Hopefully that forest is
> as dead as it looks."

Tightening my grip around the ice axe.
"Yeah. Hopefully."
And we head off into the forest.

Found and Lost (now)

"There!"

Beatrix arches back,
held up by invisible wire
like a puppet.

BAM!

Mike lets off a shot
blowing one of the three arms
off that thing.

Sprinting around Mike,
seeing the limb disintegrate
I wrangle my breath
calming my mind
and body
in the
moment.

The two remaining arms
are holding on to something...

The invisible wires
holding Beatrix?

Mind centered.

Movement of the thing
is jerky,
stumbling
sideways.

Two legs support it
and the legs bend like any animal's.
I slide toward it
ripping an ice axe through
what should be a kneecap.

Chunky blue slime explodes out of the leg
as training takes over.
I flow into a strike
to the other leg
dropping the thing
to the ground.

My body is on autopilot
sensing the creature has fallen
spinning
dropping
my axe
into its chest.

Shrieks gurgle to a death knell.

I punch down to rip
the ice axe free from whatever
bone it might have gotten caught in.

It pulls free easily
as the blue slime erupts
from the chest hole.

Life
flooding
out.

BAM!

Mike disintegrates
what was probably its head.
A pyramid
with fleshy cheeks curling around it
like a drill bit.

I breathe
to return to the moment,
calming my blood.

Beatrix is collapsed
on the ground.

Fading from consciousness.

"Beatrix!"
I kneel by her,
check her neck for injury,
cradling her purple hair
for fractures,
checking her icy eyes
for recognition.

"Can you hear me?"

"Yes,"
she says
in dreamy tones
coming back to
me.

"Are you hurt?"
I look her over
seeing white tension marks
on her wrists and throat
like wires
were wrapped around them.

She shakes her head
and tries to sit up
falling back down.

"I've gotta go."
She grabs her bag
tightly.

"Where?"
Putting my hand on her bag
knowing what will happen next.

Beatrix snaps the bag away
dropping the contents on the dusty ground.
A book.

The book from the Vault.

Everyone stops
and looks
at the book.

Each of us wanting to talk about it
but none of us knowing what to say.

Why is that?
Is it the alien world?
What happened in the Vault?
Why does Beatrix have the book
and Dr. Roderick doesn't?

Beatrix breaks the moment
shaking her head
shuffling the book back
into the bag.
"Quiet,"
she hisses.

"Quiet?"
I echo
loudly.

Mike pats the air
telling us to
keep it down.

"I've gotta go,"
Beatrix says
flustered.

"Fine. Let's go,"
I say.

"Wait, I thought
we were going back
for Greg?"
Mike says pointing
back to the beach.

Beatrix pauses for a moment,
looks around us.
"I need to get to the library.
You guys go look for him
and just catch up later."

"No way."
Branches crack
leaves rustle
just out of sight.
"We stay together."
I lower my voice.

"Fine.
But after the library,
I'm out.
Gotta look after my own."
Mike squeezes his gun
as he drops more shells in it.

Clutching the bag
to her chest
Beatrix shakes her head
and sees my eyes,
sees my intent
quickly giving up
her arguments.

"Well, then let's go
to the library,"
Beatrix says
and stomps with dissatisfaction
further into the woods.

"Great,"
Mike grumbles.
"Another library."

In the dark around us
something moves.
Too far to see,
too far to attack,
close enough to watch us.

Is it a shadow creature?

Another one of the things
Mike and I just killed?

Chasing after Beatrix
I catch Mike's eyes
and nod to the dark;
he agrees,
having heard the same thing.

We move deeper into the
black forest of this alien world
on high alert for whatever's next -
be it monsters,
addicts,
or libraries.

Oh my.

The Dealer

The forest's
leaves and bushes
are black with deep purple tips
like Beatrix's hair.

If you ignore Beatrix's white roots.
She must dye her hair?
Seems like a lot of work
to bleach it white
then dye it black
then dye it purple.

Probably another bleaching in there
somewhere.
I re-knot my own hair
keeping it out of my face.

A light gray fog
hangs at our feet
hiding anything below the ankle
as we crunch over the gravel
that snaps and pops under our feet.

I'm glad I grabbed those boots
from the supply shelf.
Clearly, those supplies
are for people to come here.

Is anyone else here?
Dr. Roderick?

"Where are we Beatrix?"
I whisper
still listening
for the rustling that was
behind us.

She jerks back toward me
snapping out of her thoughts.
"I don't know."
Confusion weighs on her words.

She turns back
to the path
squeezing the book tighter
mumbling something.

"Any guesses?"
I ask
gently.

Beatrix shakes her head.

Mike follows us
keeping his head on a swivel
looking for anything.

How can he see anything here?

The trees turn everything
murky, oily.

"Then where are we going?"
I catch up to her
grabbing her arm.
She pulls away.

"You said a library?"
I back away from her.

She nods.
"Yeah, a library."

"Why are we going there?"

"There's something there
we need to get home."
Beatrix loosens her grip
on the book.

"How do you know?"

She tenses.
"Did someone tell you?
Dr. Roderick?"

She stops.
"Did you see him?"
Her face ages
with worry.

"No? But, who else..."
I look to the book
and think about how she kept
hearing things
in the Vault.

She'd pop up
like she heard a noise
and I'm betting she did.
She heard something talking.

Checking on Mike,
he wipes the sweat
from his forehead.
"Wherever we're going
we need to be getting there."
He points to where we came from.
"Something's following us."

"Do you trust who told you?"

Beatrix looks away,
nods once,
and starts again
through the trees and branches
to the library.

She's nervous,
scared.
Inside her something says:
Don't do this.
Don't go there.
But something else,
someone else,
promises that if she does this
she'll feel good,
be stronger,
be better.

The Dealer
always has all the answers
except for how to stop.

That's one question
they never
answer.

The Black Library

As we walk through the forest
I feel grateful for
the sudden freedom.

We all need space
sometimes.
I need space
from that damn phone.

Being trapped on an alien planet
isn't all bad.

My new iPhone is pretty neat
and I love all the health apps,
but being constantly connected to SocialNet
sucks.

The trail running app,
the exercise tracker,
all that stuff is great.

I check my exercise tracker
and chuckle at the alert:
GPS not found.

Yeah, I'm living
off the grid
right now.

Way off.

News app is nice.
Having a camera at all times is cool.
I guess it is really just
SocialNet that I can't stand.

No SocialNet here.

No expectation of posts.

No worries about my mom calling me
if I don't post three times a day
asking what's wrong and reminding me
of my endorsement deals.

Yeah, that's all good.
Leaving the fake world online
for this strange world,
and at least here
there are real people.

Mike who's bundled up
in his jacket and watching the trees
like army guys in old army movies.

Tapping to open the camera app,
I snap a picture of Mike.

Beatrix who's twitchy
and nervous like she's needing
a fix.

Fix of what?

That book is bad
for her.
Whatever it did in the Vault
showed me what it means to do
with her.

Violent.

Raging.

I snap a picture of her.

The dust at our feet
turns to hardpack stone
as paving stones emerge
from the gravel.

Rustling behind us
gets closer
louder
then
stops.

Mike springs up the shotgun
taking aim into the
blackness just beyond
the closest leaves.

We all turn and wait,
watching for what's out there
to come to us.
Rush us.

Leaves rattle again
as whatever is there
rushes away
back into the
black forest.

Mike looks to me,
wondering if I heard that.
I nod
squeezing the ice axe
tight.

Phone in one hand for pictures
to remember the trip,
axe in the other for stopping
anything that wants to end it.

Beatrix is petting her bag
and staring at Mike.
Staring around him
like she's watching something.

"What do you see?"
I whisper to her.

She shakes away my question
looking down
blushing.

She was debating something
starting to reach out
but for what?

"You okay?"
I soften
and reach for her.

Beatrix nods
and doesn't jerk away
this time.

Progress?

I wave on Mike to continue
our journey to the library.
His eyes stay behind us
the gun ready.

But a moment later
we emerge from a wall of trees
facing a flat mountainside
of black stone.

Carved in the mountain
are columns and intricate reliefs.
The black stone is polished
and shimmering in the starlight.
Green marble flecks spider throughout
like varicose veins bulging,
blistering the smooth surface.

I take a picture
and gasp at the enormity
of this place.

Beatrix walks into my shot
and I see where she's headed;
the entrance is open.

"Where are you going?"
I reach for Beatrix
pulling her back.

"I'm going in,"
she says
with surprised
obviousness.

"We don't know what's in there,"
I point out
also with
obviousness.

"Claudia's right,"
Mike chimes in
still watching
our backs
standing at the edge
of the forest.

The stone path
from the forest
leads to an opening,
no door
but clearly
the entrance.

Over the door,
carved into the marble,
I read the inscription:

"Scientia est gladius et scutum"

"Knowledge is
the sword
and
the shield,"
Beatrix says.

She smiles.

She doesn't realize
she's petting her bag,
like a purring cat.

"Wait."
I pull her back again
as she tries to go in.

"I need to go."
She rips away.

"Why?"

"Just leave me alone."

"No! I want to know
what's going on."

"You want to go home?"
She stabs her chin at me.
"Then I need to go in there!"
Wild eyes pretend to be
reasonable
as she squeezes the book
into herself so hard
her jacket puffs out
and over it.

"Why!"
I'm not asking
anymore.

She's angry.

I know this face,
the 'you're standing in my way' face
from someone who needs their fix.

Unlike Jasmine,
Beatrix isn't just making a face,
boiling on the inside,
she's in my head
listening
lurking.

"Get out."
I grunt through my teeth.
"I said don't do this."

She doesn't leave.

She pushes harder,
deeper into my head.

"Get out!"

I press my palms over my eyes
to push her out
to rub her out of my mind
but she's burrowing
worming

clawing

"Hiding something?"
Cruelty drips from her.
She's enjoying this.
"Who's Jasmine?"

SMACK!

Beatrix drops.
My arm hangs in the air
still extended
my knuckles singing
from hitting her cheek bone.

The ice axe still clenched
in my fist.

People are always surprised
when they get hit.
Beatrix is no different
but she doesn't have the usual
'I can't believe you did that' look.

No, her face is
hate
searing
inferno
of hate.

Blood trickles out her lip
quickly tangling her purple hair.

"Stop!"
Mike shouts at us.

I blink hard
coming back to myself
bringing my anger
into check.

Beatrix spits
reaches for me
and I feel her fingers
slide over my brain
pushing the nerves aside
as she squeezes.

Not searching.

I drop the ice axes;
they dangle around my wrists
swinging wild
as I grab my head
trying to hold my brain inside
my skull
as she squeezes.

Falling to my knees
I scream to release the pressure
but nothing releases
just builds
compresses.

She stands over me
pressing me down into the ground.

                              "STOP!"
                              Mike screams.
                              "ST-"

He's ripped into the trees
Beatrix lets go
apology instantly washing over her.

BAM!

A shotgun blast
erupts
a scream follows...
a human scream.

Mike's scream.

I can't move.

My brain is on fire.

Beatrix reaches to the trees
trying to grab something
she laughs as she catches it
and pulls
her face
lightening.

Ecstatic
in whatever she's absorbing
in whatever is making her glow
faint pink light.

Her smile breaks
as her hand is jerked away from her.
Something has her
in one of those invisible wires.

She falls
her ankle coming up.

Another wire.

It's dragging her to the tree line.
Her bag catches around her throat.

I push off the ground
but fall
my balance
dissolved from Beatrix's grip
moments ago.

She's straining to hold on
but she's fading
her glow is fading.

Something has her.

Doing to her
what she tried to
do to it.

"Tell me what to do!"
Beatrix yells
through strangulation.

Pushing out a sigh,
I try to talk but can't.

I can't help her.

I breathe to come back
to find my center
to feel my training
but all I find is

pain

helpless

watching her die
again.

Pale.

Beatrix is pale.

Lips bluing.

Staring at me
an empty stare begging
screaming to help.

I reach for her.

Finding my axe.

"Where are you?"
Beatrix whispers.
Tears leaking from her eyes.
She's not looking at me.
She's looking in her bag.

"I'm...here..."
Breathe
climb
breathe.

The creature emerges
from the trees
sloshing sounds
from grinding teeth
as shreds of Mike
dangle from its pyramid head.

Another one of those things
that attacked Beatrix
in the forest but this time,
it got Mike first.

Beatrix flails
reaching for
her bag
the noose
dragging behind her.

My legs solidify.
I breathe
rushing the creature
seeing the hands,
all three,
holding something I can't see.

The distance between us
disappears
and I swing

too slow

it snaps me up
and shoves me toward its teeth.

I look back to Beatrix.
She's convulsing
muscles spasming
lips purple
skin ivory
twitching.

Chapter 5

The Librarian

WOHHHMMMMMMM!
Air sizzles around me
as a gush of something
blows past my head.

The creature rips in half
split down the center
by a pulse of sound.

WOHHHHMMMM!

Another streak of sound
slices the thing
diagonally and it drops me.

The ground slams my joints
knocks the wind out of me
sending the world dark
as the creature evaporates
into the gravel and dust
of the black forest.

I look to Beatrix
seeing an old man kneeling over her.

He touches her forehead
bringing her color back.
Instantly she springs up
gasping
then falls back down
quiet.

Air comes back to me
greedily dragging it in
as I claw toward Beatrix.

                              The man looks to me,
                              smiles.
                              "You're quite the fighter."

He stands
letting his blood red robe
hit the ground with a quiet thud.

His white beard
is long and scraggly
matching his eyebrows.

                              He walks to me,
                              hands up in surrender.
                              "Can I help you?"
                              He approaches like a man
                              approaching an injured animal.
                              Unsure if I'll
                              bite.

I nod.

He lifts me to my feet
with shocking ease
for an old man.

Pointing to Beatrix,
I ask,
"Is she going to be okay?"

He shrugs.
"For now."

Beatrix lies on her back
panting and breathing.

"Beatrix?"
I strain to call to her.
My head still solidifying
from her attack earlier.

She bolts up.

"I'm sorry!"
Running to me
grabbing me
squeezing my body
this time.
"I don't know
what happened!"

I squeeze her back.

Seeing her bag,
seeing the book,
everything that happened
becomes
very clear
very fast.

Junkies do all kinds of
stupid things
when their dealers
tell them to.

"Well, let's get
inside and patched up,"
the old man says.

Beatrix and the old man
hold me up
and take me into the library
where I collapse
hitting the stone floor
feeling the cold
seep into me

dark swirling
closing in
falling...

...

Beatrix Clark

Intervention

"Will she be okay?"
I ask the old man.

He shrugs.

Nods.

What happened?
What did I do?

> *What you had to do,*
> the book sighs.

> "Do you believe that?"
> The old man
> looks to me
> half smiling.

"You heard that?"

He nods slowly.

We walk further into the library
and see the gargantuan
pristine white interior.

This place must be constantly
scrubbed
to stay this white.

It glows.

Massive white orbs float
drifting around the air above us
swirling like small suns
lighting the library.

White shelves overflow
with books of all colors,
scrolls of rolled paper, some white,
some aged with the faint brown of
paper well loved, well read.

The shelves stretch into
long hallways leading
away from the foyer.

Seeing couches
and a large desk with a chair,
perhaps reception area
is more apt.

He walks toward a couch.
"I'm Brother Ephram,
librarian and
keeper of this place."
Bowing, he picks up
two white velvet pillows
from the couch.

"Beatrix,"
I say
as he takes Claudia to the pillows.
Gently he lifts her head
and slides them under.

Letting her down
he smiles
and motions me
to the couch.

I follow.

Beware,
the book hisses
quieter this time.

I follow him
collapsing on the
white couch,
dropping into its plush
like falling through
a pile of snow.

I catch myself
on the couch's arm rest
pausing as I run my hand
over the velvet feeling it
flow with my hand
seeing the shimmer
glow as the fibers shift.

He chuckles
and looks down.

I get a glimpse of a tattoo
on his bald head.
A circle,
squiggling lines radiating from it
to a solid line that encompasses
the crown of his head.

Perhaps it is a tattoo
of a star?

His lightning strands
are cropped close to his body.
They flow around him slow
like an anemone drifting
in a calm ocean.

"I keep them close."
He smiles.

"You can hear me?"

He nods.
"I won't if you
prefer me not to."

I imagine a wall
around my thoughts.
"No, it's fine.
Nothing to hide."

He leans back into the couch.
"Who said anything about hiding?"

I shift in the couch
feeling it give easily
as I rock away from him.

"No, just why else wouldn't
I be okay with you listening?"

"Privacy. Not everything is
about secrets.
Sometimes it is about control
and permission.
Giving others permission
to see your thoughts.

Trusting them
with what they find."

Seeing the wall again,
wrapping around my thoughts.
"Yes, well I'm an open book."

I smile
and focus on the wall
around my worry.
Why did I do that to Claudia?

I lost control.
I've never done something like that...

Except...

            Ephram shifts toward me,
            smiling an invitation to talk.
            "Why are you here?"

Guarding my thoughts,
thinking of
doors,
gates,
home.

"I'm looking for my professor."
Thinking about Dr. Roderick.
"Did he find this place?"

            "No. You two are the first
            I've seen in a long time."
            Ephram shakes his head.
            "Did he open the Well?"

"Yes. Well...I guess so.
It was open when I got there."

"You did not see him?
Perhaps paralyzed?"

That's oddly specific.
"No. No sign of him."
Except the blood,
the gallons of blood
from the stairs to the well.

In his mind I hear the words
Defense mechanism.

"But not the blood."
His face turns curious.
"There should not have been
any blood from the
immobilization enchantment."

Seeing my confusion,
he continues.
"The wood used for the lid
is enchanted
to grow within someone
and constrain
but not injure the person.

It only affects those who
do not belong here.
I'm guessing that you
would have not been affected,
but your Doctor
didn't belong here."

Ephram looks up,
clicks his tongue.
"No, I'd wager
someone left the Well open
and perhaps something came through,
attacked him,
and brought him here."

Ephram shakes his head
as if to say,
What a shame.

Is Dr. Roderick dead?
Where's Mike?
Is he dead?
The body count is ticking up
all because of this book...

Don't put it all on me,
the book hisses
with a trailing laugh.

You came here.
I didn't make you.

True.

I scurry behind my mental wall,
to think about how I can
help Claudia.

Stop the body count.
I think about
the artifact.
What does it look like?

"Is that what you want?"
Ephram asks
leaning back
and looking at my bag.
"Or is that what you think
you want right now?"

"The book told me
that I could go home
with an artifact here
in the library,"
I admit.

"And you believe that?"
he asks
genuine
not placating.

Ephram leans toward me
resting his elbows on his knees
looking to the floor
giving me space.
"You believe you can go home?"

Nodding.
"I hope so."

He smiles
and stands.

"You do?"

He motions me toward a desk
in the center of the room.
I follow him
to what I think of as the
reception desk.

Two books sit
on top of the desk.
"Here you have power."
He motions to the
countless shelves
crammed with books and scrolls.
"And I'm guessing you're a reader."

He smiles.
"Do you want to go home
for you
or because you think
that's what other people want?"

"Claudia and Mike
want to go home."

"Mike?"
Ephram shakes his head slowly,
solemnly in apology.
"I afraid your friend
did not survive the
pyradente attack.

I'm sorry for your loss."

I look to Claudia
melted on the floor
and motionless
except slow breathing.

Ephram's mind pictures the creature
with the pyramid head
repeating the word
pyradente.

"He's dead?"

                Ephram opens one of the books
                on the ivory desk.
                "Yes. I'm sorry.

                Were you close?"

You already know the answer.

I shake my head.

                He pauses.
                "Are you close
                to anyone?"

Claudia squirms
nuzzling deeper into the pillows.

                "Alone. Isolated.
                Hiding in books."
                He licks two fingers
                the sandpaper scratching
                of his tongue on wrinkled flesh
                giving me shivers.

The fingers swipe through pages.
"You were a prime candidate
for your book."

"What do you mean?"

Looking again to Claudia
seeing the blood in her ears
and under her nose.

Smears of red
over the white
pillows.

What did I do?

I didn't mean-
I just over-
she hit me.

I reacted.

"That book you're carrying
isn't helping you."
Ephram sits again.
He holds out the book.
"It only helps itself."

Lies,
the book roars.

Ephram rolls his eyes.
"Yes, yes.
Everyone who says
what you don't like
lies.
We've heard that before."

Ephram points to the page
showing some kind of
black cloud,
a cloud of charcoal and dust
being pulled into
a book.

The men standing around the book
in the picture all have the
same tattoo as Ephram on their head.
They wear the red robes like Ephram.
Women in white armor holding up swords
in victory surround the men
in red robes.

One of the men holds a tuning fork
that is emblazoned with golden foil.

The words on the page
rearrange into shapes
I understand.

"Binding?"

He nods.

> "That artifact you're being
> told to find doesn't
> help you.
> It helps it."
> He nods
> clapping his book shut
> sending a puff of
> ancient dust up my nose.

Lies,
the book hisses.
Anger boiling under
the S's.

Claudia starts to stir.

I move from the desk
to a shelf farther
away from her.

Brother Ephram
goes to her.
Kneeling.
Nodding.

He walks to a teapot
on another shelf
and looks at me.

> "You have choices, Beatrix."
> He selects a box
> and pulls out a spoon
> full of tea.

Turning around
he mixes the tea.

> "The book gives you one path.
> But it isn't the only path
> for you."
> He plucks two ceramic cups
> from the shelf
> with an echoing clink.

His finger lingers
over a third cup.
He looks to me,
pausing as
I watch Claudia
hearing all the things
she'll scream when she awakens.

Ephram nods
and leaves the third cup.

Claudia shifts,
waking up.
My palms sweat
my cheeks burn
I'm going to be sick.

The blood crust under her ears,
under her nose,
I did that.

I don't want to be here
when she wakes up.
I don't want to explain
what happened or
hear her say what happened
I just want it
to not have happened.

But it did.

My stomach lurches,
my throat clenches.

Bathroom!

I escape
to find the bathroom.

What Kind of Tea?

White blurs focus
into shelves
and a desk
and floating
lanterns?

The lights
don't hang
they float.

Stars.

Balls of swirling light.

                              "Hello."
                              The old man from outside
                              sits beside me
                              placing a ceramic cup
                              before me.
                              "I'm Brother Ephram.
                              Your friend Beatrix is safe.
                              Mike did not make it."

He sips his tea.

"I know."
The smell of the tea
lifts me to sitting.
Clearing my mind from the haze
of unconsciousness.

I mimic him
and cross my legs
remembering tea
with Master Oni.

Master Oni would set up tea
for me when training got hard
or when I couldn't understand a lesson

or when I couldn't focus
after Jasmine died.

Tea
transforms
you.

It can calm.

Lighten.

Drown.

Energize.

"Thank you."
I lift the cup.
Sip it.

Hot.

"No questions?"
Brother Ephram cocks his head.
"Thank you is
where you start?"
He smiles and nods
approvingly.

"I have a lot of questions."
Blowing the tea
I take another sip.
"But you saved my life.
You saved Beatrix."

His face sags
with his own questions.

"Is she okay?"
I lean forward.

"That is her choice."
He sips again.
"Her body is healthy.
Her soul is on a razor's edge."

"The book?"
I ask.

He nods,
surprised.

"I think it is poisoning her."

His mouth opens
slightly
quickly closing
leaving only a smile.

He picks up his cup,
takes a long drag of tea
and sits it down again.
His eyes never leave the cup.

                    "How did you two meet?"
                    His eyes pause on my
                    grandmother's bracelet,
                    looking puzzled.

He looks at me
waiting
for an answer.

I sip again.

"Paperwork error.
We were both supposed to have
single rooms in college
but we accidently were put
together in an apartment."
I sip again.
Exhaling the licorice taste
in a cool soothing breath.

"Accident?
Sounds like the busy hands
of Fate."
He chuckles.

"So, who is your roommate Beatrix?"

Stiffening at the comment,
I look to my tea.
"Why do you ask?"

Ephram lightens at the question,
his posture relaxing, slightly,
his face softening.

"I'm just trying to
understand my guests.
How about a different question?

Who are you?"

"Claudia."
I scan the giant room
for Beatrix but she's
gone.

"No, Ms. Bain.
You misunderstand me.
Who are you here?

Claudia Bain was who you were
back home.

Who are you here in this place?"

"I'm scared."
No thoughts
just the right words
for now.

"But..."
He sits his cup down.
It's empty.
"...not for yourself."

"For her."

"Beatrix is a big girl,
surely she doesn't need help?"
Sarcasm builds in his words
but not mean, not dismissive.

"Everyone needs help."

I finish my tea
in a gulp.

He nods.

"Even you?"

"Yeah, I guess."
My eyes drift over the white shelves,
to the arched white skeletal wood that holds up
crystal windowpanes above us.
My eyes fall to
the weathered white plank floor.

Looking
everywhere
not stopping
on Ephram's expectant
stare.

"I'm usually not the one
who needs help."

Ephram pours himself a new cup.

Reaches to my cup,
fills it
over-filling it
tea gushes over the brim
soaking into my ripped jeans.

My legs unfurl
springing me up
away from the
creeping puddle of tea.

He keeps pouring.

Does the pot end?

The tea soaks his red robe
climbing up the folds
in streams of
wetness.

"Stop! It's full."

He looks to me.
"You are just like this cup.
You are full of your past,
and now,
you spill
trying to
change the past
with more tea."

Brother Ephram points to the cup.
"Drink it
and be done
with what is spilling out
from you now."

"And what is that?"
I bite back the
indignation
but too late,
it's out.

"Anger, regret, disappointment
spill out of you.
It has for too long, Claudia.
You cannot keep pouring
those things
into your soul and expect
a different outcome.

You do not have to be
who you've been."

The pool of tea lurches toward me.
I step back

sucking in a hiss
fearing the tea's touch.

It's coming for me...
did it ever stop?

Has it ever stopped coming?

Can it?

> "Fill your cup with new tea
> but first, you need to
> empty your cup of the old tea."
> He pulls out a second pot,
> this one sky blue.
>
> The only blue thing here
> in a world of white.
> A single pot
> disrupting all that is
> around it.
>
> A white star flower
> is painted on the side.

I look at my tea
seeing the black murky dark
deep inside.

It's an infinite pit of darkness
so deep even the lights
that were dancing on the surface
have drowned in the void.

The cup is so full
my hand shakes.
Tea spills over
burning my fingers
as I lift it.

Burning me
as I hold it.

I close my eyes
and put the cup to my lips
feeling the blistering heat
smelling the bitter herbs.

"Thank you."
I put it down,
the relief of not having to drink
soothing my arm,
knotting my throat.
"But I can't."

He smiles,
bows to me.
"It will be here
when you are ready."

Standing up
I go to find Beatrix.

"Before you go,"
he says
standing
handing me
a book,
"know thy enemy."

Ephram smiles,
his eyes soft with
compassion
as he points to my heart.
"But you must also
know thy self."

I take his book,
nod, and go to look
for Beatrix.

Beatrix Clark

The Halls

Why did I do that?

I didn't want to.
It just
happened.

I couldn't stop.

Walking faster down the white hallways
stomping against the shiny floor
pushing myself further away
from what I did.

Passing each hallway,
each bookshelf
moving faster
building the space
between me
and where I lost
control.

I didn't know I was doing it
until it was happening.

> *She's fine,*
> the book whispers
> still trying to hide
> from Ephram.

I shake away
the dismissal.

No, I could have stopped.

I didn't want to.

The library hallways twist
with the edges of books,
the ridges of scrolls,
reaching out to snag me.

They want to stop me,
to send me back to Claudia
to get yelled at
to get what I deserve.

But I avoid them
as easily as I avoid
Claudia.

Each shelf ends with
another hallway.
Nowhere to hide
just more
places to
run.

I could have stopped.
I didn't.

I'm stupid
and selfish
and didn't care...

No, no. Beatrix.
You made a mistake.
It's okay.
Get her home
and she'll be fine.
You'll feel better,
the book says.

The artifact fixes all this,
it says with relief.

How?
It doesn't fix
who I am.

It doesn't fix
the machine in my head
that keeps going when
I know I should stop.

But it allows you
to do more.
And that's true.
I feel it.

Yes, that's true.
I don't lie,
that's a human thing.
It chuckles a light
comforting laugh.

Yeah, that's true.

Lies are human.

Books are facts
and stories.
Liars can write them.
But the words in them
can communicate truths
no one can fabricate.

Invoke emotions never felt,
imprint memories of others,
take you places
you could never
imagine.

Can you feel the artifact?
The book's voice smiles.

Reach out for it.

My eyes slam shut.

Denying my sight,
my nose takes over
smelling flowers somewhere
down one of the many hallways.

My ears hear the thrumming
of a string instrument,
a guitar maybe...strings
vibrating.

Opening my eyes I
see the strands of energy
flailing toward me,
rippling in the wind,
calling me.

Glowing pink light
starts drifting off me
in anticipation
of what's to come.

*Yes. Just wait
until you put it on.*

Walking faster,
accelerating
from walking to running.

My legs slow
as I hear
Claudia
shout in
another hall.

"Beatrix?"
She's looking for me.

Take her home,
the book whispers.

*She'll forgive you
when you get her home.*

I'll catch up with her
later when I have
the artifact.

I can tell her
she can go home.

> *Good idea,*
> the book says.
>
> *Keep to yourself
> until you're ready.*
>
> *She'll see
> all this is
> a good thing.*

Running faster
rounding corners
feeling the thrilling want
of Christmas morning
when I was a kid.

When the world was still good.

I'd run down the stairs
in our old house
knowing the Christmas tree
was just around the corner
with gifts and
Dad and
Mom.

After Dad died,
I had to get the gifts.
Mom couldn't think about
Christmas anymore.

The magic was gone.

But now, the magic is here
and I have an amazing gift
right around the corner.

Wonder and hunger
for what I'll find
super-charges my legs
and I sprint.

Feeling it before I see it
stopping in front of the bust
wearing it...

a necklace.

The bust is an old man
carved in marble.
A gold plate under it says:
Lost Brother Mot of Ugarit.

The necklace is metallic blue rays of light
beaming from the neck of the person wearing it;
soon it will be radiating from my neck.

At the tip of each blue ray
are gold rings
like shackles
all bound together
with a golden chain.

It's warm as I touch it
lifting it from the bust
feeling its weight
pulling my arms,
my shoulders,
me
down.

When you clasp it,
you'll be on your way
to sending Claudia home,
the book croons,
eager.

Straining to lift it
to my neck
I lower it,
looking again
at the golden chain.

So heavy.

What is this made of?
Why is it so
heavy?

It will be lighter
when you put it on,
the book grumbles
with irritation.

Do it.
You are more
with it
than you are
without it.

"Beatrix don't!"
Brother Ephram
comes around the corner.

He's trying to trick you.
You can't trust him!
the book demands.

Put it on.
That's the only way
to save Claudia.
Don't trust him!

"You don't have to."
Ephram shakes his head,
eyes softening.

He reaches for me
from across the hallway.
Calloused hands,
scarred and gnarled from
age and arthritis and toil.
"You don't need it."
Ephram tenses,
his eyes asking
for a different outcome.

Humans lie,
the book hisses.

*You can't get Claudia home
without this.*

I need to get Claudia out of here.

I need to make up
for what I did.

*Yes.
Make up for what you did.
Do it.*

Ephram's head is still shaking
as it falls in despair.
He knows the discussion is over;
perhaps it never could have
gone another way.

I latch the necklace
with an echoing
CLICK.

Threads of gold lightning
slither from the necklace
and wrap around me
in a hot crackling energy.

I explode in a pink pulse
releasing the electricity building in me
knocking Ephram down.

My body drifts
up off the floor,
pushed away from the ground
by pink wisps of energy
whipping off me.

Yes, I feel the power of the artifact,
the necklace flowing through me
and the book did not lie,
I am powerful with it.

I'm awake.
I've been sleeping
my entire life
with only hints of
what I could do.

Now I know.
This has always been there
I just needed to wake up.

And now I am awake.

Now I'm alive.

the book shouts over
the vibrating air
engulfing me.

"Beatrix, I cannot let you go,"
Ephram shouts.

I laugh
at the old man.

I am alive
for once
fully alive
fully charged.

"I'm not asking.
Move."

Floating toward him.

He blocks the hallway.

"Beatrix, don't do this."
He raises his hands
stiffening his fingers
preparing for...

the book warns.

"Last warning."

                              "And for you,"
                              he says.

Let's see what
fully charged can do.

Doors

Ephram's hands
tighten around silver threads
appearing at the tips of his fingers.

Not his strands of lightning...?
Where are those coming from?

He flicks the silver threads.

WOHM!

A slice of energy
rushes toward me
and shatters on
the gold lightning
swirling off me
from the necklace.

The silver strands in front of him
still vibrate with a fading
wohm-wohm-wohm.

I smile.

He flicks again
more strength in his fingers
this time
sending a louder pulse.

WOHHMM!

Another slice
explodes toward me
digging into my light
like a nail working
through leathery skin.

Still smiling,
I grab the white strands
from the balls of light
floating in the hallway.

I push my energy
through the threads,
a whizzing pink surge
erupting from me into the light spheres
turning them from white to pink
and bursting them
in an explosion of molten light.

The blast throws Ephram
down the hall
slamming him
out of my way.

"I said move."

The book laughs
echoing in my head
as I float
toward the exit.

"Beatrix!"
Claudia calls
panting as her running
echoes down some distant
hallway.

She's close.

I can take her home now.

No! Don't stop,
Come back for her.
Open the door
so she sees you
didn't mean
what you did
to her.

Remember what you did?
Remember how you hurt her?

Yes, what I did to her.
I didn't mean it.

It was an accident.

A faint chuckle follows.

Yes, that's right.

Flying out the library entrance
I feel the threads vibrating
from the stone circle.

Earlier I couldn't feel them,
but now, I wonder
how could I have missed them?

Their throbbing pounds inside me
like the bass beat
from the Vault...

Mike's bar.

Right...
Claudia needs to go home
and I need to show her
I'm not that person
who hurt her.

It was an-

       -accident,
       the book croons to me.

I nod
then race along the black forest
following the pulse of energy
calling to me
from the stone circle.

The Climb

Not far from the library entrance,
I find stairs twisting up
the side of the mountain.

Floating upstairs
for the first time
on a mountain with no guardrail
seems pretty stupid.

I let the energy under me
fade and my feet return
to the ground.

> *Best to save your energy*
> *for what's up there.*

"What's up there?"
I bite my lip
looking back to the library entrance.

Should I wait for Claudia?

> *No!*
> the book snaps.

> *I mean, there's nothing*
> *up there you can't handle*
> *alone.*

I start to climb
the crumbling,
ancient steps
worn down
to rounded
corners in spots.

The book cheers me on
as I get winded from so many stairs.
Pausing to hold the stitch
in my side
the book pushes me on.

Don't stop now!

Don't give up like you always do.
You're almost there.

I nod.

Do I always give up?
Why did it say that?
Maybe I do give up
and just never
noticed it?

The stairs keep going up,
so do I.

Huffing for air.
Feeling my heart about to burst
from exhaustion
and all this power
straining to get out.

I climb on.

Falling to my hands and knees
near the top.

Clawing up the last stairs
gasping for breath
in the thinning air.

I look back to the forest
so far below me now
it stretches forever along the horizon.
I can see the water beyond
the forest,
and through the grayish mist
of the horizon another mountain
rises from the black waves.

No sightseeing!

Let's go!
You're almost there.
Don't give up now.
You can't save Claudia
if you're a quitter.

I nod.
I'm not going to quit.

I'm not going to quit.

Crawling up
the last stairs
I collapse on my back
and look to the stars
weaving through wisps
of green nebulae.

My head rolls to the side
as I suck in all the air
I can find up here and

see it.

The stone circle.

I stop breathing
as my eyes are blasted by
the madness of this
twisted Stonehenge.

The stones morph, bulge, and flex
like they're made of solid tar
that can't decide if it is
stone or water.

>*The door home,*
>the book sighs,
>its voice spiking at the end
>with eager glee.

"I can save her."
I nod
and sit up.
"I'll send her home."

>*Yes, let's go home Beatrix,*
>the book coos.

>It pants,
>hungry,
>voracious.

>*Let's go home.*

Home

"What do I do?"
I stand up
legs still wobbly
from the climb.

Approaching the stone circle
the changing stones
curling open for me
to enter.

Once I walk in
they re-form
with a shloomping noise
closing the circle.

A gray slab is in the center
of the circle with a mandala
etched deep into it.

I stand inside the mandala.

It feels right.

Inside me
the energy gurgles
and rolls.
I double over
seeing my pink light
growing brighter.

"What's happening?!"
My stomach tenses
and I grab it
trying to pull out
whatever is stabbing into it.

*The portal knows
what to do with you,*
the book says
with an eerie calmness.

*This will pass.
It is attuning to you.*

Strands of pink lightning
dangle from me
flowing into the ground
pouring my light into the mandala carving
filling it up
igniting the symbols around me
to glow and pulse with life.

Threads of lightning
rise from the mandala and
entwine with pulses of energy
pumping from me
into the stones.

They pull my energy
charging themselves
draining me
but more power flows
from the necklace.

The blue metal
dangles from my throat
as teal light
slithers out
replacing the gold light
that protected me,
now cocooning
my body.

They tighten
constricting around me.
Can't breathe...

> *The door is opening,*
> the book cheers.
>
> *Focus! Focus on prying it open.*

I strain to look
seeing the air in front of me
bubble, boil, and blister.
A sliver of sores form
like a zipper
popping open
leaking thick white liquid
dripping away to reveal
a rip in the world.

Small at first
it stretches
into a wound
open and bleeding white,
bending and twisting the light,
my light,

the world's light,
as it strains to open.

PUHHWAHHHHH!

The wound rips open
into a small tear.

Black smoke rushes around me
in a vortex of frozen air
weaving through the pink lightning
coming from me,
then dives into
the wound.

I look into the hole
seeing what a surgeon must see
when they split a body open
writhing cords and tissue
bulging and rolling
bleeding light not blood.

Drips of glowing white leak
and pool on the ground
under the opening.

The fleshy purple beyond the tear
gushes a stream of liquid light
as something stretches the wound
splitting the rip in reality
with a wet fleshy shredding sound
as it pushes through.

Red smoke rises from the wound
stretching out,
solidifying into a hazy
patch of bloody outer space.

Stars twinkle in the red,
as three legs, two in the front,
one in the back,
unfold from it.

Each leg is made of scales
that look like broken glass,
jagged and hungry to shred flesh,
almost transparent
with a tint of red.

Each leg ends with three claws
sinking into the ground
a few feet away from me.

As it rises,
stands,
a spiral galaxy winks open
in the center of its body.
Stars, dust, shattered worlds
spin around a black hole eye
wreathed in flaming red light.

"What…"
Can't talk
my throat strains
as the energy is ripped out of me.
I'm sucked dry from the stone circle.

Need to pull away.

> *NO!*
> the book shrieks.
>
> *You're almost done!*
> *Don't fail.*
> *Don't quit.*
>
> *Don't hurt Claudia again.*

But…
that isn't home…

The thing that was birthed out of the rip,
that thing doesn't look like anything
from home.
It's shadow and broken glass.
It's red smoke and bloody space.

It reaches for me
with three finger claws as it
props itself up on
that tripod back leg.

> *NO!*
> the book growls.
>
> *Leave her!*
> *She's mine!*

But it doesn't listen.

It grabs me,
one broken glass claw wraps my throat
with slicing, shredding ferocity.
The other hand twists into
my pink lightning strands
snapping them from the stones
and starts to drink deep.

It drinks from me
as I drank from the scorpion snakes
but there isn't much left in me.

The stones drank so much of me,
now this thing gorges on the rest.

This close I can smell the greed
radiating from the red smoke creature.
A smell so deep in my nose,
it scratches my throat
dragging retches out of me.

I want to puke
but nothing comes.
No matter how hard
my stomach pumps
nothing comes.

My stomach twists
the necklace's chains cut into my skin
I'm going to die here.

I'm going to die.

I'll never see my mom again.

I'll never be who I could be.

Judgement.

Judgement for what I've done.

What I did to Claudia.
What I didn't do to save Dad.
I'm going to die on the same day
he died...

Tears splatter the gray slab
under me in dark splotches.
I can't die now.
Can't quit.

My guts turn
tightening
each crank
twinging to
snap
as they twist
into a ball of
energy.

Energy.

Deep in me
where my guts turn
and heave
there's something more
than pain
than failure
there's

light.

It's inside me like an egg
and I tap it,
crack it,
light shining through the shell
bursting out
as I feel the charge
erupt from my core
turning my light
from faint pink to
vibrant purple
rushing from me
to the stones
they stop shifting
turning solid
turning purple.

The broken glass hands
snap away from me
yelping
in shock
and fear,
yes, fear seizes the
spiral galaxy eye
making it gape and
retreat from me.

I scream,
crushing my eyes shut
pushing everything I have out of me.

Opening my eyes
hearing paper ripping,
seeing the wound in reality
opening big enough
for Claudia to climb through...
if she were here.

I look for her.

She's not here.
White light drips from my mouth
splashing on the mandala with
sizzling splats.

A roar of rushing wind
comes from the wound
dragging my eyes to it
seeing something coming.

The black smoke is returning
from the gory insides
of this world.

But the smoke isn't
just smoke anymore.
Inside the smoke are
broken glass arms and a leg.

The spiral galaxy eye opens
and angles toward me
hungry,
wanting
the meal its red smoke monster friend
didn't finish.

The smoke monster turns to the rip
and screeches a fear drenched cry.

WOOOHHHHHMMM!!

The monster is blown back
into the dripping wound
catching the edges
before it goes all the way in.

I collapse from the force
of whatever hit the creature.
My face hits the stone slab
cold and hard.

The world starts going dark
as the ground shakes
and Claudia calls to me
from far away.

She screams from
a long hallway
far behind me
getting longer
and longer
as the world goes
darker

and darker

until the dark
devours me.

Chapter 6

Deception

"Beatrix!"
No answer.

That vibrating sound
I heard when we first found
the library...
when Mike died,
when Beatrix almost died,
comes again.

WOHM!

Softer than it was before.

I run
toward the sound
still feeling the
reverberations in my teeth.

The white shelves
angle and curve
creating a labyrinth
of bulging books
and scrolls.

Each turn
results in another shelf
or another turn.

WOHHMM!

I pause,
feel the vibration
in the floor
and run toward the source.

POP!

SISSSSS!!
An explosion,
sizzling,
Ephram shouting,
grunting.

"Beatrix!"
I scream through
the fear bubbling around
what's happening.

Another one of those things
from outside?

Is something attacking us?

Or...

I sigh as
the scene solidifies
in my mind.

It's Beatrix.
She did something.
The book told her
to do something
and-

Coming out of a turn,
I see Ephram on the floor
trying to get up.

"Ephram!"
I rush to him
but he waves me off.
"What happened?"

"Beatrix's mind
has been poisoned."
He grunts and climbs to his feet.
"The book is manipulating her.

I feared this would happen.
I wanted her to choose herself
over the offers of the book."
Ephram shakes his head,
huffs a disappointed sigh
transforming it into a
calming breath
as it flows out of him.

He waves for me to follow.
I do.

Rushing to the front of the library
where I first woke up,
Ephram starts scanning the shelves.

I put the book he gave me
back on the desk.
Checking the spine, in silver letters
it says:
The Book of Binding.

"Is this the time for a book?"
I run to him as his fingers
flow over the spines on the shelves
jumping the scrolls crammed
between leather covers.

He nods.

                    "Most certainly.

                    In times of conflict
                    knowledge should
                    drive action
                    instead of action
                    driving knowledge."

"Know before you go."
I smile, remembering the cartoon
that use to say that.
Saturday mornings with Jasmine
and our babysitter, the TV.

He nods.

Ephram's brow crinkles
into a thousand sand dunes
between the canyons of his temples.

Lighting up
when he plucks a book
from the shelf:
The Book of Doors.
He takes it to the desk
in the center of the room.

"You must get Beatrix out
of this place."
He runs to the couch,
quick for an old guy.
Grabbing another book.
"This place,
The Rim,
is amplifying her power."

He pauses his flurry of motion
looking at me
and I see a lesson
forming on his face.

I know this look,
the 'listen carefully' look
I always got from Master Oni
before a hard workout.

"Beatrix is gifted."

I nod
agreeing to the obvious.

"She's naturally attuned
to the resonance of reality.

Everything in all worlds
has a frequency to it.
There are energies she can see,
she can feel

that are the flow of this
frequency."

I nod
listening carefully.
The definitions of the words
tie together in a sensible meaning
but I don't understand.

"She can..."
He grabs the air.
"...hold the energy
and manipulate it
which will eventually
allow her to do..."
He chuckles.
"...amazing things."

He pauses again,
returning to the books
on the desk.

"There is an entity trapped
in the book she carries
and it is trying to escape.

Beyond the book, other entities
here will feel her power
and try to take it for their own.

Her resonance is powerful.

And it can be taken,
just like she has taken
resonance
from others already."

I nod,
feeling the deck of cards
in my pocket,
remembering
the card trick back home,
how easy it was for Beatrix
to manipulate
what showed on the card.

That's nothing compared to
what she can do here.
She glows with power,
she doesn't do card tricks,
she doesn't entertain,
she rips the life from things
she attacks.

She attacked me...

"What happens if her
'resonance' is taken?"

> "She will become
> out of frequency
> with reality
> and cease to exist."

Not die.

Sounds like death would be
a better outcome.
At least when you die
you go to the afterlife but here,
in this outcome,
it sounds so
final.

Let's not find out.

"How do we leave?"

> He runs to another shelf.
> "There is a doorway home
> in the basement of this library.
> With *The Book of Doors*
> you can go home,
> but make sure to
> leave *The Book of Doors* here.
>
> You ought not to come back here..."
> His face furrows
> between threatening and
> mourning.
> "...nor anywhere else.
> Just home."

He stops to make sure
I received his message.

"*The Book of Doors* stays here."
I nod.

> "Beatrix's power will be
> sought by many entities
> in other worlds.
>
> Your world is dangerous enough.
>
> The other worlds..."
> He stops,
> shivers.

Ephram takes a deep breath
as he rushes to the door.
He pauses at the teapots,

taking the blue teapot
and putting it on the desk
with the books.

Not looking at me
he nods
and looks to the entrance.

His eyes turn
hard, unflinching;
the years, the real years
of his life appear
under and around those eyes
through the folds of time
and dehydration.
He's older than I thought,
perhaps older than
this library.

"I need to help her,"
I say.
His eyes are not those of someone
who wants to help Beatrix.
They are the eyes of a man
ready to stop her.

                      "I know.
We must do
what Fate requires of us."
He sighs,
eyes turning sad.
"No matter what we
might want to do."
His eyes drop to my ice axes
as I pick them up.

He nods,
his face hardening
through sadness.

We run out of the library
to find Beatrix.

Stairs, Rips, Whispers

Sprinting alongside the mountain,
I gasp again at how fast he is
for being so old.

I can barely keep up.

We come to stairs
sticking out of the cliff
going up.

Pink lights
flare up
at the top.

Ephram runs up.

I follow.

Thankful for
Master Oni making me run
bleachers.

Grumbling at these heavy
boots I grabbed from the
shelf by the well.

Stairs crumble under us
as we run.
Ephram's bare feet
silently sprint up
gaining distance on me
as my boots clop
against stones
slipping on rounded edges.

Almost there
I'm losing steam
but Ephram accelerates
hearing something
I can't.

"Run Claudia!"
he barks.
"No time to be tired!"

He doesn't lose a step
to demand more of me
and I respond.

Panting.

Running.

The steps go straight up
hardly any angle;
it's more like sprinting
up a stair climber
than bleachers.

"Prepare yourself!"
We're almost at the top.
My legs are starting to buckle.
"We arrive for battle!"

What does that mean?

It's just Beatrix up here?

As we crest the steps
I freeze
seeing Beatrix on her hands and knees
heaving breath, growling through pain,
glowing drool cascading from her lips,
the world ripped open and something
racing toward us,
rocks like Stonehenge
changing their shape and glowing
with purple streamers wrapped around them.

Ephram doesn't lose a step
tightening his hand
like he's getting ready to play
a bass guitar.

"Beatrix!"
I scream
and find my sprint again.

                              "Be gone!"
                              Ephram booms
                              his voice shaking the ground
                              as he plucks the air
                              like a guitar string.

WOOHHHHHHHHMMMM!!

Energy explodes from him
splitting the air
with a sizzling shockwave that
blows something I don't see
into the rip.

Red smoke stretches out from
the rip in the world.

It looks like the thing
from the Vault
but red instead of black.

The red smoke rushes out the stone circle
running on three glittering mosaic legs.
It vanishes down the stairs.

Running between the moving stones,
Beatrix collapses.
I grab her limp body
pulling her into my lap.

"The necklace!"
Ephram runs to us
waving his hands
pulling something toward him,
gathering something he can feel
in the air around us.
"Take it off her!"

I pull at it
but it doesn't come loose.

His hands work fast,
weaving unseen strings together
into a tapestry.
He's working the energy
he told me about.
The energy that Beatrix
was stealing from others,
that was being stolen
from her.
"The clasp!"
he shouts.

Grabbing the clasp
I click it open
hearing glass crack
rattling to
a roar of malicious whispers
coming from the rip in the world.
Pulling the necklace from her,
her glowing stops
the lights around her
dry up.

She shivers
and moans
stretching out
to sleep.

Ephram ties a knot in the air
with deft hands
that slowly lower.
The rip closes
with a soft puff.

Whispers continue
rage dripping from the sounds.

Beatrix's bag.
The whispers are coming
from the bag,
from the book.

Twist

Ephram doesn't talk.
He scoops Beatrix up
and carries her down the stairs
taking large steps to avoid
the glowing white liquid
in the mandala.

I follow.
Looking back
seeing the stones
shrink and bulge,
stretch and twist
as we leave.

Their black surfaces
catch the nebula's greens
in ripples like the moon
on a pool's surface.

Ephram carries Beatrix
over his shoulders
like a fireman
carries a child.

She bobs lifeless
with each step.

Her eyes flutter
and jump in
nightmares.

We leave her bag,
the book from the Vault,
at the stone circle.

Keeping it away from her.

She'll want it back,
but those stairs
are a good deterrent.
Too difficult to just run up,
plenty of time to doubt
or be talked out of
using again.

I sigh at the thought.
Is there a far enough distance
or steep enough climb
that will deter her?

The necklace is still in my hand,
at the foot of the stairs.
I should have left it too.
Clipping it to my belt,
I'll keep it close
and steel myself for when
she asks for it.

Because she will.
She'll deal,
negotiate,
plead.

And she'll yell,
scream,
bark,
say things
designed to hurt,
designed to make me
not care.

Steel myself?
My steel is
battered,
heated to the point of folding,
tired.

I want to say fine, go, do it.
Live your life,
I'll live mine,
but I've seen that story.

It has a shit ending.

In the library
Ephram places Beatrix
on the couch.

Her face is blank.

If her eyes were open,
staring at me,
she'd look like Jasmine
when I found her.

Limp.

Ragged breathing.

Will a seizure be next?
Spasms?
Foaming mouth?
Twisting arching spine?

Jasmine was on a concrete floor.

Her body jumped
and twisted so hard
she probably broke bones.

Jasmine choked
and gasped for air
hacking through vomit
and vodka.

Needle sticking out of her arm
broke in one of her
twists.
The sounds of
glass cracking,
metal snapping
against the concrete floor
always fill quiet moments
for me.

Ephram stands with me
holding my hand
as I wait for
Beatrix to spasm
to twist
to hit the floor
with cracking bones.

I listen for her jaw to tighten
clenching so hard
her teeth splinter.

But she doesn't move.
She's quiet.

I hold up the necklace
and look at it.
It is beautiful
but the gold shackles
scream the purpose of this
isn't to empower
but to enslave.

Jasmine once told me
when she was high she could
meet people's expectations.
How did Beatrix feel with this on?

Ephram lets go of me
and goes to Beatrix
picking her up again.

I drop my ice axes
near the door
lightening myself
to help with Beatrix.

He takes note
wincing as he picks up
Beatrix.

"The Garden is where
her soul needs to be
right now."
He smiles to me
and carries her.

"Perhaps a stop
at the Alter of Clmal
would be in order for us,
my dear."
He smiles
with sympathy
and motions for me to follow.

Tears sting
and surface
from wounds
I'd hoped were
drowned
deeper.

But no.

Some hurt is a geyser
never waiting
for its time,
always ready,
always building,
always bubbling.

Bursting.

I follow him.

Altar of Clmal

Quietly
following Ephram
he motions me to
wait while he lays
Beatrix in the Garden.

I peek into the entrance.

The Garden is green
and fresh
and lush
and a place where anyone
would want to wander.

The ceiling opens
to a blue sky,
not black stars.

Ephram rests Beatrix down
on a bed of white star flowers.
She curls into them
her eyes instantly calming.

A blissful sigh
pushes out of her.

Ephram plucks a flower,
tucks it into his red cloak
with a deep cleansing breath,
then leaves the Garden
and motions me to follow.
I check on her again
as I pass the entrance.

She's still.

Sleeping.

We don't talk
through the twists of shelves
when Ephram stops,
takes another cleansing breath,
smiles, and goes into a room.

I follow but he stops me
holding up a palm.

                    "Shoes."
                    He nods to my feet
                    and smiles.

"Oh..."
I kick off the boots.
"Sorry."
Giving him an apologetic smile
as I remember Master Oni reminding me
'Don't forget your shoes.'

I spent so much time on the mat
in Master Oni's dojo
that I always forgot my shoes
when I left.

Maybe I knew where I belonged back then.

Stepping into the room
with Ephram my eyes are instantly pulled up
by the massive white pillars
stretching to a ceiling
so far from us
I get dizzy trying
to see it.

One giant silver wire clock hangs
from a silver chain
at the top of each pillar.
Seven pillars, seven clocks.
All but two are at midnight.

A deep blue banner
hangs at the far wall
pointing to an altar
chiseled from blue and gold marble.

Ephram walks up to the altar
runs his fingers over the
carvings
and smiles.

I follow him up
noticing the room is
totally empty
except the altar,
banner, and columns.

I expect pews
or benches
facing the altar
but there's nothing

except white marble floor
with the occasional gray vein
breaking the monotony.

"This altar is where
all Brothers of Clmal
are given our robes."
His hand flows down his red robe,
"And are sworn to their
oaths."

This close
I see that the carvings
in the altar
are words in some
unknown language.

He grips the sides of the altar.
"Part of the oath
is leaving
who you were,
who you should be,
and what you've done
behind."

He smiles.
"I said the words,
meant them,
but leaving yourself behind
is not something easily done."

I nod
and look back
toward the Garden
wondering if Beatrix
has awoken yet.

Or is she seizing
and we're not there?

I step to the door.

                    Ephram opens a book
                    on the altar.
                    "The Brothers of Clmal..."
                    His voice booms in the hall
                    bringing my attention
                    back to him.
                    "...protect the Veil.
                    You cannot be distracted
                    in this task.
                    Doubt,
                    regret,
                    wishes
                    can be the temptation
                    used by the things
                    within the Veil, and
                    in the Lands Beyond,
                    to lead you astray."

                    He pauses,
                    tracing his finger
                    over something in the book.

"Are you the last?"
I ask him
approaching the altar.

Where are the other brothers?
I've only seen Ephram
and only evidence of one person
with one desk,
one chair,
one couch.

He shakes his head.
"No, there are more."
Ephram fingers through pages,
stopping on one.
"I'm the last here
but others are scattered.

I am a member of
the Keepers of Knowledge,
the Order of Xacary,
and we wear red to remember
the cost of that knowledge."
He motions to his cloak again.

"There are other orders,
but we all share
a purpose.

We protect against
entities like what is
in that book."
He taps the book.
"They threaten balance."

Coming to him,
seeing the page.

"The Lightless?"
These words I can read
but the rest are jumbled
on the page.

"Banished from the
Lands Beyond,
the Lightless devour
matter and energy.
They're voracious
and the Veil is their prison
keeping them
between our world..."
He motions around us.
"...the Rim,
and the Lands Beyond."

"What are the Lands Beyond?"
I look closer at the book
seeing illustrations telling
the story of the Lightless.

"That,"
he sighs,
"is a much longer conversation."
Ephram taps the open page
for me to look closer.

Words, more art than writing,
are jumbled and mixed in a language
I can't read.

The illustrations are clear,
the red robed Brothers of Clmal
joining with women in white armor,
a great war against smoke creatures,
building of a wall.
"Is this the Veil?"
I point to the wall.

He nods.

"So, the Lightless came here
to the Rim then the Brothers
and these ladies
made the Veil as a prison?"
Pausing to look at the white armor
encasing women of every shape,
size, color,
glowing on the page.

A question popping into my mind.
"Wait? Then who banished them here?"
I ask.

He shrugs.
"We don't know.
The beings that exist
in the Lands Beyond
are both timeless
and as alien to us
as we are to an amoeba."

He turns the page.
"We do not know their purpose
but sometimes,
we are caught in their
machinations.
The Lightless being banished here
on the Rim is one example.
There are many more."

My eyes drift through the pages
of the book,
seeing illustrations of people glowing,
of strings coming from people and animals.
The Brothers are shown as protectors,
keepers of the library and other
buildings.

Ephram sighs, deep, tired,
sad.
"I must go and prepare
a few things."
His head drops
in a solemn nod.
"You should go see Beatrix
but before you do,
take a moment to read this page.
It could help."

I look at the page.

Five words are legible:

Know thyself now not then.

"Think on it."
He nods
and leaves
back toward the
Library entrance.

"Wait!"
One more question
comes to mind as he leaves.

Ephram turns back
welcoming the pause
with a relieved smile.
"Yes?"

"The book Beatrix has…"
I think of the bag
by the stone circle.

"It's called
The Garden and the Well."
I smile.
"I get the well. It's a door."
Thinking of Beatrix.
"But what is the garden?
Is it a place of healing?"

Ephram winces.
"No."
He shakes his head.
"Our garden here
is not the garden that book
speaks of"

He shivers.
"That garden is not as..."
Looking down, finding the word
with a grimace.
"...pleasant."

I nod
and he moves on
to wherever he was going.

Looking back to the altar,
I feel the carvings like Ephram did.
They're sharp,
hard
and deep.

Know thyself now not then.

I go back to Beatrix.

Beatrix Clark

Hello, again

Flowers?

The soft
fresh
smell of flowers
is all around me.

Opening my eyes
to sunshine
and green.

A garden?

Did we get home?

Sitting up,
stretching.

How are you feeling?

I turn to the door
but no one's there.
"Hello?"

Beatrix, I'm still here,
the book says
with a wily smile.

Where is my bag?

They left it behind
thinking that would
leave me behind,
the book whines.

Grabbing my neck,
it's gone.

"Where's the necklace?"
Remembering how
heavy
it was.
How it pulled me down
and filled me up.

Feeling so full,
so much energy and power.

It was heavy
but
I could handle it.

Claudia has it.

Frustration drips from the book.

She's not wearing it.

Disappointment.

Just carrying it around.

"What happened?"

An unfortunate oversight
on my part. I'm truly sorry.

Is it sorry?

You were over-charged.
I didn't know you were so
deficient
in channeling your abilities.

Deficient?

I just realized I could do this...
yesterday?
Two days ago?
I think it's been two days...
How long have I been here?

Hopeful thinking that I could
just do it,
just use this new ability,
led me to
stretch too far.

If I were better
Claudia would be home now.

We'll work on it
together,

the book says
supportively.

But you're going to
need the necklace back.

I nod.

I need the necklace.
I need the book.

Yes, they help me
focus.
My bones tingle
with the vibrating power
of the necklace
as it comes closer.

Heavy boots clop along the hallway
and thoughts of worry,
worry about me
come with them.

It's Claudia.
She's coming...

Realities Collide

Should I start with
apologies
or
demands?

Saying I'm sorry for
what happened in front
of the library

or

telling her to give me
the necklace
so I can open the way home
again?

Was that the way home?

> *Yes,*
> the book answers quickly.
>
> *That was the way home.*

I nod
and remember
when Mindy died.

After she committed suicide,
I read our favorite book
every night until I could sleep.

Bedtime came with chapters of
Ender's Game.
We used to read it together
on the phone
and I felt like I was going to sleep
talking about the book with Mindy
just like when she slept over.

Books helped me
process her death.

And after Dad's accident,
I'd read Mom the poems
he loved,
the words of Langston Hughes,
and we'd think about him
cooking, singing.

Books helped me then too.

Let me help you again,
the book pleads.

*Get the necklace
and let's go home.*

Claudia comes around
the entrance
and smiles when she sees me.

Her perfect teeth glittering
her silky black hair sparkling
the sunlight here glowing
on every perfect feature
of her perfect face.

A SocialNet perfect face
but the imperfections emerge
with a longer look.
Crumbling dark brown crusts of blood
leaking from her ears,
from her nose.

Torn jeans are
soaked and caked with
black mud.

Black skid mark bruises
line her shins
where she must have slipped
on rounded stairs
when she was running up
to me.

"Good thing you grabbed that coat."
I smile at her.

           "And these stylin' boots."
           She twists in a practiced
           fashion model curve
           highlighting her dusty boots.
           "This place isn't made
           for heels."

Those high-rise stiletto heels
wouldn't have lasted long here.
Between the gravel,
the mud,
the sand,
she'd have been barefoot long ago.

           Claudia's brown eyes
           look me over.

On TV, she'd be my older sister
straightening my hair
or rubbing my shoulder,
showing how much she cared
while helping me through
some tender moment.
"How you feeling?"

But there's no tenderness here
just the need to get the necklace,
the need to feed my power.

So I can get her home.
That's why.

Coming back to her question,
I shrug
and look to the sky
not sure how to answer
wondering if the answer is
somewhere up there.

"Sore.
Tired."

Dangling from her belt loop
the necklace sings
as the blue beams of light
clang together like wind chimes
welcoming me home.

I point to it.

She shakes her head.

"It isn't yours."
Pointing out the obvious.

            "Or yours."
            She smiles
            dismissive.

Gathering my thoughts,
preparing my debate.
"I can open a doorway home
with that necklace."

            "How did you know about this?"
            she asks
            and walks into the Garden
            leaning on a tree.
            "The necklace?"

"The book said it could help."
Going with honesty
to establish the credibility
that I have the answers.

The book has given them to me.

"I can hear the book
in my mind.
It has been helping me
understand my abilities."

She doesn't react.

The words just drift between us.

                    "How do you know
                    it isn't helping itself?"
                    Claudia comes closer
                    sitting with me in the flowers.
                    "You were in real bad shape
                    up at that circle.
                    Did it do that to you?"

"No,"
I answer quickly
to dismiss the idea.
"No, I just overdid it.
Just lost control.
I know what to do this time.
Won't happen again."

She laughs
throwing her head back
gasping laughter
building tears in her eyes.

                    "Yeah…"
                    She wipes her eyes.
                    "Yeah, I've heard that before."

She takes a deep breath.
I want to know what she's thinking
but hold off listening.
I want her to trust me.

"So, so…"
A despair-stricken sigh
leaks from her.
"…so many times before."

I look away from her
to avoid my impulse
to look in her mind.

She won't notice,
the book prompts.

I shake away the thought.

"You want to go home,
then I need that necklace."
Emphasizing my point.

Reason will reach her.

"Ephram says there are doors
in the basement here that will
take us home."
She moves closer,
reaching for my hand.

"I don't trust him."
Returning to her eyes
the urge to read gone
now the urge to warn
taking over.
"Something about him
just isn't right."

Why didn't he help sooner?
In front of the library,
why didn't he stop that thing
from killing Mike?

He should have helped,

the book agrees.

He didn't want to.
He wanted Mike gone
so you two would be his.

He's going to try to control you.
He's probably
controlling Claudia now.

She's going to try to turn you
against me.

Be careful.
He's poisoned her.

"Yeah, he came in to save us
but where was he when Mike needed him?"

That hits her.

I follow up,
"And if we can leave
why doesn't he just take us
to these 'doors'?

Cause he wants us here
and helpless.

So, let's get out of here.
We can go while he's not around
and escape. I can get you home
without him if you-"

"Just give you the necklace?"
she finishes my statement.

And pulls away from me.

"Well, I need it to open the door."
Nodding at the obvious.

She sighs,
connecting dots
that I wish I could see
without her knowing.

"Okay, okay..."
Putting up my hands
in surrender.
"You carry it until
we get to the circle.
And if you think things are
getting crazy, you can have it back.

I promise."

The last word
sparks her
eyes.

Claudia stands up
the necklace
swinging to me
as she moves to the door.

She wants
the necklace
for herself.

"It won't work for you."
I scoff at the idea
that she'd try.

"I don't want it,"
she bursts
screaming at me
face red
neck bulging.
"I know a junkie when I see one!"

Stabbing her finger at me
driving in vicious words
her thoughts screaming at me.
"My sister promised too!
She made deals,
she made arguments,
and they all seemed reasonable
until I found her with a needle
in her arm choking to death on her own
puke."

A bathroom floor,
blue tiles, diamonds,
white walls,
marble sink, bathtub.

A girl, Jasmine, looks like
Claudia but sick and strung out.
She jerks and flops on the tiles
white froth streaked with brown vomit
erupts from her mouth.
A volcano of death.

I'm at the door
seeing this
screaming for help.
Two people are behind me
Jasmine's 'friends'
and they run.

I'm alone.

What do I do?

Screaming for help again
no one comes.
Someone from down the hall
shouts at me to shut up
their voice crackling out of a fog.

I go to her.
Kneeling.

I can't find my phone
in my pocket.
Hands don't work to get it.

Jasmine looks to me.
Her eyes
pleading for help
her mouth moving
spitting the mixture of death
onto my cheek.

Then her lips stop.

Her pleading eyes stop
settling in a look of
apology.

Jasmine dies.

I cry.

I beg.
No, no no please no.

Squeezing her close
feeling her warmth fade
as the stench of letting go
fills the room.

> "You'll be next,"
> Claudia says
> returning me to now.

Palming the tears from my eyes,
clearing my blurry vision
seeing Claudia not angry,
but resigned.

Her eyes aren't sad,
they've giving up,
dropping like her shoulders
and head
hanging heavy
with failure.

"No...I-"

Someone grabs Claudia from behind
falling on her
as she twists away.

The attacker falls to the floor
his tweed jacket flipping up
exposing muddy faded jeans
and scuffed loafers.

"Dr. Roderick?"
He looks up,
sighs, and nods.

The Doctor is In

We pull him to the flowers
and he rolls over.

Clothes are ripped,
face beaten and bloody,
hair caked with gore
as are his hands.

"What happened to you!?"

Don't trust him,

the book says.

You say that about
everyone.

Red marks cover his throat
like he had been strangled
with a wire...
just like my wrists earlier.

Claudia checks his neck,
his head,
looking for obvious injuries.

Thoughts of a class
where someone is showing her
how to check for injuries
in an unconscious patient
float up in her mind.

The teacher is wearing a blue t-shirt,
LAFD EMS in white letters
on the pocket.

I look away to leave her.

"No injuries
I can see."
She pulls open his eyes
looking into the irises
pulling back quickly.

"What?"

She looks at him.
Shakes her head.
"Nothing.
Thought I saw...
something."

"Dr. Roderick,
can you hear us?"
I call to him.

Rousing, he sits up
slowly coming around.
"Where...am I?"

"A library."
I point to the greenery.
"This is a garden
in the library."

Dr. Roderick looks around
taking in the Garden.
His eyes drift up
to the blue sky
and look puzzled.

"I think it's an illusion
or something.
That's not what the sky
really looks like here."
I smile.

Claudia backs away,
her eyes still red
from our

discussion.

She leans against a tree
near the entrance
looking out.
Keeping guard.

"What happened?
How did you get here?"
I ask.

Dr. Roderick wraps his arms
around his knees and
takes a deep breath.

The Strange Case of Dr. Gregory Roderick

Did something in the well take him?
All that blood?

I try reading his mind,
hearing nothing but static.
A fuzzy white noise
I've never felt before
from someone's thoughts.

Claudia watches him.
Analyzes him.
She steps out
of the Garden and looks
down the hall.

        "How did you get here?"
        she asks.

Her posture,
her eyes
are all on
high alert.

        "I was attacked."
        He stumbles over the words
        finding his voice.
        "And I ran away."
        Dr. Roderick's eyes
        wander toward the entrance
        as he raises his bloody hands
        examining them.

"I found this place
and came inside."

I lean closer to him,
seeing him twitching
as nervous energy
ripples through him.

"Yeah, we found this place too,"
I agree
reaching for his thoughts
to see what else happened.

Static again.

He must be in shock.
I guess getting attacked in an
alien world would do that.

"Someone was at the desk,"
he says
his voice flat
as he puts his hands down.

"Ephram."
I nod.
"He's the librarian I think."

Claudia looks out to the hall,
her eyes jutting back
to Dr. Roderick, and then
walks out of the Garden.

"Claudia and I were just
about to get out of here.
To head home,"
I tell him and he looks
concerned.

"Ephram says there are doors
here that will take us
home."

the book warns.

I know,
don't trust Ephram.

Dr. Roderick's face
drops with concern.
"The only way home
is through the stone circle
above this place."

He sighs.
"I think this Ephram person
is lying to you."

Yes,

the book concurs.

"That's what I was thinking too."
Relief blows over me.
I'm not the only one.

Claudia has good intentions
but she's too trusting.

Too eager to see the good in people.

                              "Let's get out of here,"
                              he says.

"But Claudia won't give me
the necklace I need
to open the portal home."
Before the words are done
I try to snap them back.

I'm not a weirdo pretending.

"I mean, a lot has-"

                              "I understand."
                              He smiles.
                              Nods cold and certain.
                              "I'll get it.

                              I'll go talk to Claudia,"
                              he says, struggling to his feet.

"Did you hurt your legs?"
His knees give out
like a toddler learning to walk.

                              "Just old."
                              He laughs.
                              Forced and uncomfortable.
                              "The necklace?
                              Why do you need that?"

"It amplifies my powers.
The book told me about it."
Sitting taller
thinking about
how we could talk
about all we learned.

Laughing, I imagine a class session
where all the idiots are debating
what we've learned here.

They wouldn't understand,
why bother telling them?
They'd grumble and whine
at the chance to learn
to be anything more
than average.

                              "Okay,"
                              he says, curious.
                              "I'll talk to her.
                              Wait here."

He goes out the door
and I sit in the flowers.
Taking a deep breath
to pull in their sweet smell
but all I smell is rot.

The flowers
where Dr. Roderick was sitting
are all dead.

Chapter 7

Claudia Bain

Binding

Where is Ephram?

Something isn't right here.
Dr. Roderick lost all that blood
we found in the library
back on Curson Street.
That would have left anyone
in bad shape.

Not wandering around
and fighting off
the monsters
we've found here.

Beatrix hangs on every word
but something isn't right.
His pulse was too slow.

His eyes too dilated.
And I don't think I just imagined
the red fog moving in his eyes.

Muddy footprints trace
back the way he came.
Beatrix can handle herself
if needed.

I follow the footprints
through the halls.
They stumble and stutter
like Quinn after
a night at the club.

The muddy loafer prints lead to
the entrance of the library where
Ephram lays crumpled
over his desk of books.

Rushing to him,
I peel him back
as his stomach stretches
and his insides spill out
on the floor.

I jump back
dropping him.

He hits the floor
with a squish.

Beside where Ephram lands,
my axe is coated in blood.
I left it here

when we got back
from the stone circle.

Someone caught him
by surprise.
Axe to the back,
then too many hacks
to the gut.

Unnecessary hacks.
Rage filled hacks.

Ephram...

I kneel beside him
picking up his hand
feeling the icy dead flesh.

"I'm sorry."
Tears drip onto his fingers
as I wrap them around mine.
His fingers have blood
on the tips
but no blood
on the rest of his hand.

I stand and
see the bloody letters
scrawled on the desk
by one of the books.

CLAUDIA

Going to the desk,
looking at the book
with blood on it,
the page he opened
for me to see.

It is another illuminated manuscript
of red robed, tattooed heads,
Brothers of Clmal.

The bothers are pulling
what looks like a spirit
out of a man.

A golden pitchfork
is guiding the spirit
out of the man
and into a book.

On the page,
written in Ephram's blood,
is the word

Binding.

Spirits being bound
to people...
to books?

Looking at the spine,
I see the silver lettering,
The Book of Binding.
That's the book he handed me
earlier...

"Quite the mess, eh?"

I spin to see
Dr. Roderick
slumping hunched,
smiling at me
with a vile grin.
The blood
on his hands
isn't his.

"The necklace. Now."
He points to the
blue and gold metal
swaying around my hips.

I breathe
knowing what comes next.
My blood pumps,
my mind calms.

One step to the axe,
three steps to him,
I see the attack.

He smiles.

"Last chance. Give me
the necklace.
Let Beatrix and me
walk out of here."
He points to the entrance.
"You let her go,
you live."

That's bullshit.

I'm surprised
he said that without
laughing.

Deep breath,
cleansing breath,
emptying my mind.

Beatrix collapsed on the slab in the stone circle.

Deep breath,
cleansing breath.

Beatrix turning blue outside the library.

Deep breath

Jasmine in the bathroom.

"No!"

Stepping to the axe
reaching for it,
it flies into his hand
I don't stop
rushing him now
seeing my target

seeing Jasmine choking

my throat slams into his palm
my feet jerk out from under me
his hand closes around my neck
lifting me
squeezing
breath
out.

Kicking at him
nothing lands
just bounces off.

I smack his arm
but it's like iron
so I claw at him
ripping
his flesh like paper
but no blood
just red smoke...
and broken glass scales.

It *is* the red smoke from the stone circle.
It rolls and twists around
inside the flesh suit
that used to be
Dr. Roderick.

He laughs.

Opening his mouth wide,
ripping the flesh that attaches
his lips to his cheeks,
jaw unhinges
to the size of my head
and sucks.

But whatever he's trying to drink
isn't there.
A dry gurgling
surprises him
disgusts him
and he squeezes
my throat.

I scream;
only a whimper escapes.

This isn't it!

I kick
and claw
ripping away the rest of his arm
but the red smoke holds me up.

Can't breathe.

Limbs heavy
clawing
kicking
breath gone

rage fuels me now
I'm not dying like this.

I have to save her!

He lifts me higher
my eyes sore
as blood vessels pop
lips numb

vision dark

Beatrix!

In the hall!

Nothing.
Did she hear me...?

I have to save her.
Can't die.
Not like this...

throat tight

no air

dark.

Beatrix Clark

Red Smoke Rival

Was that a scream?

Claudia?

I reach out to her mind
and see Dr. Roderick,
choking her.

*Get the necklace
before he does!*

Sprinting to them
I go out to the hall
confirming what I saw in Claudia's mind.

Dr. Roderick holds her up
with a broken glass arm
and red smoke.

As if she was waiting for me arrive,
Claudia stops kicking
stops fighting
limbs falling lifeless.

He slams her to the floor.

"Claudia!"
I reach out to her mind
but it isn't there.

Dr. Roderick walks to Claudia's body
flipping her over with his foot.

"Get off her!"

He doesn't stop.

"You're not Dr. Roderick!"

                  "You said I was Dr. Roderick."
                  It laughs.
                  "Doesn't matter now.
                  I needed his form
                  for this."
                  It grabs for the necklace.

"Enchanted artifact
for enhancing resonance..."
Its hand stops before touching the gold
chains.

"Where's Dr. Roderick!?"

"Dead."
It laughs.
"Worm shit by now.
I found this body mostly eaten
in the black forest
and took his form.

Didn't know it would be
so useful."
It giggles.
"Thought I could sneak in,
steal your resonance
and return to the circle
but now..."

He looks to the necklace.
"Now, I'll do so much more."

Red lightning
peeks out from
the crimson smoke.

Reaching for its strands
they grow toward my hand
lashing at me.

I snag them
and drink greedily
but it laughs and
rips me toward it.

Throwing me
smashing my face
as I hit the stone floor.

"Amateur,"
it scoffs.

Its red smoke encircles me
grabbing the strings around me.
Pulling my energy
a feeling that's getting too familiar.
"You're a feast."
Dr. Roderick's face grins
too wide with ripped lips
smiling at me as if a joker
in a deck of cards.

Smiling.

Laughing
at my stupidity.
Laughing
at the fool
who thought they could
be more.

That isn't your teacher!
Stop it before it gets
the necklace!

The smoke throws me
into a bookshelf.
The shelf stops my chest
my legs whip around
my head cracks
against another shelf.

Darkness pops;
white stars
bring my vision back.

"Claudia!"
I call for her to help me.
She's been helping me.
Why isn't she helping me?

Her body lays on the floor.
She doesn't jump
to my rescue.
Doesn't run to help.

My gut twists
and drops
falling with the hope
that Claudia's still there.

The necklace is your only way!

Dr. Roderick reaches
down to Claudia,
grabbing the necklace
pulling it up
dragging her lifeless body
into the air.

It shakes her
trying to pull the necklace free,
trying to toss her aside like
flicking mud from your fingers.

"Let go of her!"

Get the necklace!
The book's focus is only
on the necklace.

But all I can see
is Claudia shaking
like a broken puppet.

She can't be gone.
She can't be another person I'll lose
if I don't do-

A glowing silver strand
appears in front of me.

Not Dr. Roderick's.

Not mine...
just a strand out of nowhere.
Like how Ephram flicked the silver strands
to throw energy at me...

Pluck it.
The book's breathless command
begs me to comply.

I grab it,
the strand solidifying as my finger
hooks into it.

Plucking the string
a burst of energy explodes toward
Dr. Roderick ripping his body apart
leaking red smoke out.

WOOHHHHMMMM!

Another thread appears.

And another.

They've been there
I just couldn't see them.

Plucking and pulling
and sliding and ripping
waves of energy explode from me
but the cloud reforms after each
slice.

It rushes me.

I jump away
slamming into the desk
in the center of the library entrance.

The red smoke grabs my strings again
pulling harder.
Sucking the energy from me.

Pulling me closer
to the center of the cloud,
the spiral galaxy eye gleaming
with delight.

Laughter ripples through my mind;
it's laughing
at me.

I strain against it
but can't move.
This is how Claudia died,
except her air was stolen.

My lifeforce is being stolen.

Grab it!

the book shouts
hard in my mind.

Electricity, remember!

I grab the smoke
feeling it solidify in my grip.
Drinking,
gulping,
gorging on the flow.

Energy loops through me
going faster and faster
as the red smoke sucks my energy
and I suck the energy from it.

I'm glowing.

My pink light drowning
the white fireballs around us
as we float up
higher and higher
twisting into
a vortex of light and
bloody smoke.

The smoke pulses and squirms
trying to escape
but I hold on.

The short circuit is created.

I feel the energy
coil in my guts
charging my battery
charging every nerve in my body
to life.

It pulls away
releasing my strings
but I hold it firm
drinking faster
dissolving the red smoke
in my shell of light.

Trying to escape
the red smoke,
its broken glass arms and leg,
it goes to run
but I hold it
absorbing the last drops
of life
in whatever it was.

The smoke vanishes,
the broken glass appendages
shatter to nothingness.
The spiral galaxy eye
collapses on itself
vanishing.

I float down to the library floor
and kneel at Claudia's body.

Trying to reach her again,
finding nothing,
no thoughts,
no static,
no Claudia.

"No..."
Digging deeper to find her.
Pushing my mind into hers.
Pressing my forehead to hers
but nothing is there.

No one is there.

No Claudia.

My light fades.
My tears break free
falling on Claudia.

I'm alone.

I unclip the necklace.
My eyes apologize
to Claudia
but my mouth can't
form the words.

The necklace isn't as heavy
this time.

I put it on.
No surge.
Only a numbness
that now seems infinite.

No power will shine through this
emptiness.
Nothing but nothingness
is in me.

I've done enough here.
Enough death.
Enough failure.

It's time to go.

Doors Revisited

The stairs
are not as exhausting this time
perhaps because
you can't make a well any more dry;
you can't get more exhausted
when exhaustion is all you have.

The stone circle
accepts me in.
My feet stop at the center
of the mandala in the
gray stone slab.

Looking at the necklace,
I see my bag,
the book,
tossed to the side.

Picking it up,
I put on the bag
and go back to the slab.

"Home."

Indeed.

Just like before.
Open the door.

"Just like before."
I drip my light into the slab
illuminating the carvings.

Pink lightning threads
explode from me
racing out to the stones
and slithering around them
with eager embraces.

Gulping like before,
draining me
pulling it all in,
the necklace's strings
unravel and strangle my body
drinking every drop of energy
I have left in me.

The rip opens,
easier this time?

No.
Not easier.
I just don't care.
What's left?

I couldn't save Dad.

Or Mom.

Or Mindy.

Or Mike.

Or Claudia.
The body count climbs
as I stagger through life.

Opening wider
ripping farther
the black smoke from earlier
races toward me.

Something's with it.

Both things birth from the rip,
stretching it open to make room,
spilling into the world
with a wet splat.

Glowing white liquid splashes from
the wound in the world
in a gushing splatter.

More energy flows out of me.
I'm slobbering the same
glowing white liquid that came
from the wound.

It splashes on the mandala
and streaks over my boots.

My gut twists again
feeling the well going dry
like trying to suck the last drops
of soda through a straw.

Three appendages unfold
from the black smoke:
broken glass arms and a
back leg.

Each ending with three claws
stretching into the ground
as the smoke lengthens like a cat
who just awoke from a nap.

The smoke encircles one of the stones
and the wound seals with a puff.
I'm still draining.
Something's wrong.

Coming toward me,
I can see inside the smoke.
Seeing the stars within it,
a purple nebula floating within it
like a scar on the perfect dark.
A spiral galaxy eye winks open,
the black hole in the center
warbling with a
frequency that
spins my mind
with the galaxy's glare.

"Home?"

> *I am home,*
> the book says.
>
> *Well…closer anyway.*

The creature made of stars
reaches a broken glass arm
toward my bag.
As the arm stretches,
it grinds with a
glass-on-glass screech.

It pulls the book from my bag
and throws it in front of me.

The pull burns
straining to rip everything from me.
I try to let go,
but I can't.

The stone circle pulls harder.

> "We're done with that."
> The voice no longer
> comes from the book.
>
> No longer in my mind,
> now coming from the creature
> in front of me.
> The black hole in the eye
> pulses with the voice.
> "But not quite done with you."

"Home?"

I whimper,
tears darkening
the gray stone slab
now glowing under me.

> "You didn't want to go home,"
> it says.
> "But I do.
> You let me come back here.
> It is a first stop
> for me to go home."

My light fizzles.

Sputters.

Fails.

I'm empty.

I fall.
Exhausted.

"Wha…"

"I told you,
you're a battery
and I needed a lot
of power to get back here."
The smoke creature laughs
like shattered glass
falling over metal.

Its eye rattles
with malicious glee.

One of the arms
reaches for my neck,
those glittering talons
swiping along my neck
unclasping the necklace.

Slinging the necklace around itself,
donning it like a sash.

The blue streaks of metal
stab toward me,
the golden shackles dangling
in my eyes.
"A binding totem."
It laughs.
"When you put it on
you gave in to me.
You gave me your power,
your potential."

"No..."
I whimper.

Too weak.

"Yes.
A loner like you
didn't need any convincing.
You only trusted
books.
Lucky me."
It laughs
peeling back from me.

"I've been looking for you
for centuries,"
it coos.
"And now, with your
resonance,

I'm going to rip down the Veil
and go to my real home."

The creature drifts to the edge
of the circle.
Stepping outside it
with a triumphant cheer.
"Without the Veil, my people
will feast on the worlds from here
to infinity.

And being trapped so long,
we are

a hungry lot."

"Used me..."

Tears fall.
Muscles strain to move.

"Used..."

"Don't be so dramatic.
It was good sometimes, right?"
it says in a pouty voice.
The black hole in its eye
sagging in a grotesque
tragic mask.
"I used you.
You used me.
We all got what we wanted
in the end.
I get to escape.
You get to be alone."

No...

The creature glides away.
As it does,
my strength returns
but I can't feel anything inside me.

No energy.

Nothing warm
or good.

Just

nothing.

Nothing Left

Crawling down the stairs
I go into the library.

Can't look at Claudia's body.

Or Ephram's.

From Ephram's desk,
a book beside a teapot has fallen.
Picking it up,
I see
it is *The Book of Doors*.

He must have been looking at it
when he was killed.

The killer.

Dr. Roderick's paper flesh
lies deflated on the floor.

This place is a tomb.
The white walls
strewn with scars
and burns from our fight.

Blood slicked floors.

Decay.

I can't be here.

Turning to leave,
but where would I go?

To the forest?

To the water?

Wherever the black smoke went?

No, I want home,
and there's only one place
like that here.

The Garden.

I follow Dr. Roderick's footprints
back to the Garden.

Seeing the dead flowers,
knowing now that I was too
focused on the necklace
to see the obvious.

Now it's too late.

The tree where Claudia was leaning,
she probably saw the flowers
or something that told her
things were off.

At the far end of the Garden
is a statue.
Poseidon maybe?
The statue
holds a two-pronged gold trident.
A bi-dent?

I sit at the statue
and page through *The Book of Doors*.
Ephram was right.

There's a room in the basement
that has doors to everywhere.
This book shows how to navigate them.

Doors that lead to
the Veil,
the Rim,
the Core Worlds.
Some pages are ripped out.

Reading about each,
seeing
the Core Worlds
is what Claudia was talking about.
Home.

Our home.

Ephram was trying to help us.

I believed the book
over the people trying to help me.
Claudia.

Ephram.

Mike.

All dead
because I didn't listen.
Because I wanted
to do it myself.

Now, I'm stranded
on the Rim
alone.

The book was right.

I got what I wanted.
What I deserve.

To be alone.
Everyone is gone because of me.
Because I failed.

Sliding down
balling up.
Like a baby I let the
sorrow come.

Screaming into the sky
to the statue
begging to know
what to do now?

Screaming until my throat
goes raw and the copper taste
of hopelessness comes up
with each howl.

What do I do?

Scratching footsteps
come from the hall.
The dragging
sliding step
of some broken thing
is coming.

Probably one of those things
that killed Mike.

I just lie here.

I've got nothing.
No power.
No weapon.
No will.

It groans
and falls
through the door.

It's Claudia.

III

The Bitter,
The Sweet, &
The Apocolypse

Chapter 8

Not Dead Yet

Crying?

Screaming?

Shaking the fog away.
Breathing strained.
Throat bruised.

Susurra's bracelet hot on my arm.

"Hhhh…"
Can't talk.

Clenching my fingers,
trying to
pump blood
back into my hands
trying to get them
to work,

to come back
to life.

My wrist burns.
The beads on my bracelet
bubble and roll in the scorching
waves trickling up my arm
down my body.

Clawing
at the marble floor
pulling myself toward
the scream.

A woman's scream.

My fingers find their strength
around the throat of my ice axe.
My legs find their
stability, enough stability,
as she screams.

Dr. Roderick's body is deflated
on the floor; she must have stopped him.

There's blood on the bookshelves.

The necklace is gone.

Hard to stand.
I push along the wall
down the hall
following the sobbing.

Panting as I go.
So tired.

Sliding down the wall,
using the axe as a walking stick
pushing to get to her.

"Ja-"
I try to shout
but it's not her.

Jasmine is dead.

Stopping, sliding down the wall,
"Jasmine..."
I croak through my throat
remembering her eyes at
the end.

Apologetic eyes.
She was sorry.
Why?
For what she did?
For what was happening?
For what she was leaving me with?

Guilt.

Anger.

Memories.

The final mess I had to clean up?
The mess in me
for everything that could have been
different.

"Beatrix..."
I whisper through strained chords.

Falling through the door,
I try to raise my axe
to fight
but can't stand.

Beatrix is crying at a statue.

She runs to me
and squeezes me
screaming apologies
and drenching me with tears.

The necklace is gone.

Her eyes are Jasmine's eyes
but alive.
Is this what would have been
had Jasmine lived?
She would have screamed sorry
until she couldn't talk.

Beatrix squeezes me,
rocking me.
I look up
seeing what Jasmine would have seen.

Her tears were my tears.

Past the rain of tears,
past Beatrix's purple hair
suffocating me,
my eyes drift
to the statue.

I gurgle a laugh
through a broken throat.

Did fate tell her to sit here?
Did Ephram show us this place
to prepare for what's to come?
The statue Beatrix is crying under
holds the Fork of Binding.

The golden two-pronged pitchfork.
It's a tuning fork.

Laughing
convulsing laughs
choking on the humor.

Ephram was right;
Fate's hands have been busy.

Alone

Beatrix tells me
of the fight with Dr. Roderick,
the book's deception,
the necklace's true purpose.

I nod.
Still can't talk.

No surprises
in her story,
in being used,
being discarded
after you served
your purpose.

"You should lay
in the flowers."
Beatrix helps me to them.
"I think they heal
or something."

She takes me to the flowers
that aren't dead
and lays me down gently.
"Do you feel it?"

I do.

Instantly
feeling a warm
surge inside my soul.
"Yes."
My voice returns,
crackling as my throat
realigns from strangulation.

"This is amazing."

My bracelet burns again,
the beads shift
and grow
and...glow...
but I'm just
imagining that.

Shaking my head,
getting my senses back
into alignment.
I look again...
no glow.

Must have just been
too much time
without oxygen.

Seeing things.

That's all...

                              "I thought you were dead?"
                              she gasps through tears.
                              "I couldn't feel you
                              and when the book said..."

"It was isolating you,"
I grunt.
"Knew it needed to control you."

She looks away
cheeks blushing.

"Stupid."
Beatrix shakes her head,
more tears coming,
sour frustrated tears.

"No. Just human."
Holding her hand,
I squeeze.
"You wanted to be more
and it promised you that."

"And now it's going
to destroy everything
just to get home."
Anger boils up
out of her embarrassment.

"Not if we stop it."
I sit up
feeling my muscles loosen
and regain their strength.

"Ephram showed me a book
that talked about this."
I point to the Fork of Binding.

"We can use it
to put that thing back
in the book.
Or...anything we want."

"But how?"
Beatrix waves her hands
in confused swirls.
"I don't have anything left."

She believes that,
but I don't.

The card trick at the apartment
happened before the book.
The fork can be used
without it too.

Maybe she just needs
a moment to find her
power.

Maybe a break?

A tea break.

Beatrix Clark

Tea and the Witch

We go into the library lobby
still spotted with bodies
and blood.

Claudia rushes to a specific shelf
pulling out two mats
and two blue
porcelain teacups.

"My old karate teacher,
Master Oni,
used tea as
a meditation exercise,"
Claudia says
throwing the mat open
letting it drift down
to the floor.

She sets a teacup down.
"Ephram showed me
where his tea stash was."

"I don't know, Claudia.
I've tried meditation before
and it doesn't work for me.

I can't stop thinking."
Stepping to the mat,
I pick up the little blue cup.

"Don't try to not think.
Just go where your mind takes you
and let it go."
She sets up her space
and rushes to the desk
to get the blue teapot.

She stops at the desk
her hand hovering over
a white cup
still steaming.

How long has that tea been there?
Why is it still so hot?
I hear it bubbling
with little pops
tossing tea into the air.

Claudia grabs it
and brings it to her mat.

"Okay. I'll try."
She sets the teapot
on a hot plate
and it starts to warm.

We sit
and she starts breathing
loudly
in

hold

out.

                              "Breathe to focus."
                              She relaxes instantly.
                              Her white cup sits steaming
                              a blurring mist
                              hiding her face.

I copy her breathing
and smell the tea
as the pot whistles.

Sweet scents float up to me.

She pours into my cup.
The tea is not nearly as hot
as hers but is warm to the touch.

It's so sweet
like it was boiled with
honey or perhaps those flowers.

Those flowers that smell like

hiking with my dad
in the woods.

I'm in the woods.

"Don't push away thoughts,
just go with them,"
Claudia says from far away.
"Let them drift away
when they are ready."

A path winds through the woods.

Dad isn't with me anymore.

These trees are green
but dark.
This is thick forest,
alive, not dusty and dead
like the forest outside
this library.

The trees are tall
and intertwine at the top
making a web of branches.

Snapping twigs
and crackling leaves
under my feet
release the smell of
old woods,
mildew, and
moss.

"Explore the thoughts,"
Claudia says dreamily.

Singing floats in the air
and I go to it.
Smelling sweet
cookies
baking.

How do I know that smell
is cookies?
I just know.

A house.

A cabin in the woods
with the door open.

The walls twist and roll
like lollipop tops,
curve and tangle
like candy canes.

If I were to lick the wall,
would it be sweet?

The cookie smell comes from inside,
inviting me in with the
smooth silky chocolate taste
slipping into my nose.

The doorknob is gold
with a
six-petal rose
delicately
engraved on it.

I go in.
The door doesn't creak
as I push it open.

A rocking chair creeps
and squeaks
slowly rocking
back and forth.

A lady sits in the chair.

A metronome of motion
squeaking slowly on the backswing
slower still as she comes forward.

She sings in a language
I don't understand.
Maybe if I listen closer,
I can?

Walking toward her,
following the cookies' scent,
she stops rocking
but keeps singing.

She knows I'm here,
she's singing to me.

Her fireplace crackles
welcoming me to come closer,
the cookies are blossoming on a tray
over the flames,
her song steady and light,
dreamy.

Rounding her chair,
I see a cascade of silvery white hair
flowing to her knees.

A braid dangles to one side
more like heavy rope than hair.
She flicks it away and
looks to me slowly,
calmly, a loving smile
blossoming on her face.

The smile doesn't crack the paint
on her face.
A light blue stripe across her eyes and cheeks,
a crescent moon where her third eye should be,
her eyes are white
but not scary, just
surprising.

She's beautiful
but not young.

Intoxicating
but not
blinding.

"Well, aren't you interesting,"
she says with a joyful smile.
"Lost?"

I can't talk,
I just shake my head.

Am I lost?

Maybe I am?

I shrug as a final answer
looking away
not worthy of
seeing her,
being seen by her.

"Never think that, my dear."
She reaches for my hand,
I pull away from her
light,
her kindness.

She takes my hand
quick as a hummingbird.
"Oh, where are my manners.
I'm not use to
unexpected visitors."
She pulls cookies from the fire
without a mitt.
"Cookie?"

They are the
gooey
delicious,
the unreality
of a commercial.

I take it from her.

As I touch it,
the cookie starts
melting in my hand
pooling around my fingers
in white liquid light.

"Well don't just look at it,
cookies are made for eating."
She giggles and leans back
relaxed and full of life.

I pop the remaining cookie
in my mouth making sure it
doesn't fall though my fingers.

That'd be rude.

My eyes close
to savor the taste.
Hot chocolate
mixed with sugar cookie
and...

What is that flavor?

I lick my fingers,
sucking the chocolate
tasting glowing light
off them.

So amazing!
Keeping my eyes closed to savor it,
to discover it,
to let my body explore the texture
and taste and feeling.

What is that flavor?
Not chocolate...

"Power, my sweet."
She takes my hand again.
"That taste is your power
and no one, no thing,
can take it."

My eyes open
to see her
but she's gone.
I'm at the library
where Claudia is holding
her cup of tea.

Her eyes fall so far
into the tea that
this place,
her cup,
even the tea
no longer exist
for her.

She is alone
with the tea.

Tears drip into
the black tea,
splashing up
biting at her fingers
with a quiet sizzling
burn.

She breathes out a long breath
and drains the cup in a savoring sip.

Claudia exhales a long
sigh of white smoke.

Smiling,
she puts the white cup down
and pours the blue pot to refill her cup.

        "Would you like some?"
        she offers,
        her eyes lighter
        than before.

"I would."
She pours
and I sip
tasting the cookie again.

Smiling.

The cookie filled me up.

My light
begins to glow.

The black smoke said
it took everything.
I guess it didn't know
everything I had.

Neither did I.

Preparations

After the tea,
we both stand.
I wrap my arms around Claudia
squeezing apology and appreciation
into her.

She squeezes back.

"I'm sorry."
The words are cleansing.

Claudia nods,
squeezing me tighter,
tries to pull back
but I keep her close.

"This is great and everything
but we need to move,"
she says.
I step back from her.
"I'm guessing that smoke thing
isn't waiting for us to stop it."

"No, I don't think it is."
We laugh.

"Do you have any ideas?"

She nods,
picks up the meditation mat.
"Yeah, I do.
We'll bind it to this mat.
And then drop the mat
to the bottom of the ocean."

Meditation mat?
Seems kind of
anticlimactic but
we'll use what we have.

We go to the Garden
and get the tuning fork
from the statue.

It takes two hands to carry
but only one to swing it.
I jab and slice the air with it
thinking about hitting the smoke.

Claudia shakes her head
and motions me to follow.
We go to Ephram's desk
to get *The Book of Binding*.

I review the text
which reshapes into words I can read.
The words are incantations
to use when striking what you want to bind
and more words to seal the binding.

After the incantation,
the book explains how
the sounds of the words
and the tuning fork
create a frequency that
resonates with the strands of the world
and the strands of the thing being bound
creating a harmonic resonance.

The harmonic resonance
creates the binding
until it is broken.

Flipping the page,
looking for
how it is broken...

But there is nothing.
So how did the creature in the book
get out?

What happened in the Vault
that let the creature out
of the book?

"You charge at it with the fork."
Claudia snaps me back to now
holding out the golden
tuning fork,
more spear than fork.
"I'll sneak around and jump on it
with the mat. I'll wrap it up
while you do, you know..."
She points to the book.
"...the binding stuff."

"How do you know if
I have my abilities back?"
I ask,
doubt growing thick.

The plan is simple
but it relies on me
being able to do this binding.

What if I can't
without the necklace?

Without whatever
that thing took from me?

"You can do this."
Claudia holds my shoulders.

"You could do this magic stuff
before the book."
Reaching to her back pocket,
she pulls out my tarot deck.
Gray backed cards,
golden line art.

"You could do stuff then,
you can do stuff now,
you'll do it after we bind
that monster, learn more
when we get home
and get better than ever."
Her confidence boosts me.

I nod
hiding the
doubt.

"Where would it go
to tear down the Veil?"
I look to the shelves.
"Probably a book about that here."

But there are so many books.

Books beyond books,
it would take centuries
to find a detail like that.

"Ephram made mention of that."
She waves me to follow
and we run to a giant hall
with massive white pillars
and a brilliant blue altar.

Claudia runs to a book
on the altar.
"Here, it's the story of
the Veil."
She points to the page.
"But I can't read it."

I can.

The words re-form into
letters I know.

"It says,"
I start,
tracing the words,
paraphrasing to keep things quick,
"the Veil's power source
is in the Temple of the Veil."

"Where's that?"
Claudia flips through the book
looking for a map.

Closing my eyes
I reach out for
a power source.

I felt the necklace,
maybe I can feel this too?

But I don't.

I knew
I couldn't do this
without the necklace.

                        "Could we use
                        The Book of Doors?"
                        Claudia asks.

I think back to the book
and remember that the doors
work on location and intent.

If you know where you are going,
you just need to think it
when you step through the door.

I nod.
"Yeah, I think that could work."

Claudia rolls up the mat.
I tuck the Fork of Binding
under my arm.

We head down to
the Room of Doors
where Ephram wanted us to go
a lifetime ago.

"For luck."
Claudia hands me
the tarot cards.

I nod.

"Well, go on.
What's going to happen?"

"Doesn't work like that."
I knock on the deck
and grab the top card
peeling it up.

A dark feeling runs down my spine
stopping my hand.
Dad said to use these
to find my way,
but I don't want to know
where I'm going this time.

Because it's not a good place.
Bad feelings about the future,
today – ten years after his death,
these feelings in me now
are those feelings all over again.

Putting the card back,
shoving the deck into my jacket.
"Let's just wing it,"
I say

and nod away
this feeling that won't leave.

A feeling that this
is a one-way trip
for one of us.

Claudia shrugs,
nods.
"Works for me."

The Room of Doors

Through the halls,
down the stairs,
and the Room of Doors
opens to us.

A rectangular room
with four doors
lining each side
of the long room.

Eight doors in total.

According to the book,
the doors on the left,
the entrance doors,
used to come to the
Room of Doors.

The ones on the right
are the exit doors
used to leave the
Room of Doors.

Each door is associated
with a plane described in
The Book of Doors.

Each door has the destination
carved above the doorframe.

One door for the Core Worlds,
one for the Veil,
one for the Rim,
one for...the name above the door
is etched off,
the handles on both sides of the room
flattened
and unusable.

"Guess those are
out of order."
Claudia chuckles
uneasily.

"We want the Rim.
That's where we are now."
I point to the door.

It is black
with an oddly angled frame
and a dark purple
doorknob.

"Core worlds?"
Claudia says.

"Home."
I nod.

The white door
and gold handle
is tempting.

Home
would be nice.
Mac and cheese,
maybe even mayo mac and cheese
would be good right now.

I go to it.
My hand holding the
golden knob.

"Not yet."
Claudia gently
pulls my hand away.
"We have some
cleaning up
to do
first."

She nods.
"Both of us."

Going to the Rim door,
I grab the handle.
"Think of the Temple of the Veil
when I open the door."

She nods.
"Just say the words in your mind."

"Ready?"

"One."
I twist.
"Two."
I push.
"Three!"
We step through.

Exits

Still walking
I pause
seeing our surroundings
have changed.

Looking back,
there is no door.
Just Claudia looking
confused.

My hand is still holding
the doorknob that isn't there.

We look around,
seeing that we're outside
in a vestibule
leading into
the temple entrance.

Above us,
the gaseous nebula
yawns hungry
casting the large, ruined columns
and archways around us
in pale green light.

Claudia's hands
squeak as her grip
on the ice axes
tightens.

She breathes
calm
focused.

"Where is it?"
Claudia whispers.
"Can you...
feel
it?"

Reaching out
with my mind,
I do feel it.

I feel the necklace
calling me to come.

Yes, Beatrix,

the black smoke creature's voice
whispers into my mind.
I'm here.
Come to me.

"Yeah. It's here."
I nod.

We walk toward the entrance
through the webwork of vines
that ensnare the columns.

Moss and fungus
reach up the columns,
entwining their broken archways
high above us.

Maybe once there was a roof here
but that has long since crumbled.

Broken reliefs
spot the ground around us
where the ceiling caved in,
showing the scenes
from the Veil's construction.

Cloaked men gather,
energy encircles them
growing into an egg
blocking out monstrous cloud-like forms.

The ground was once white stone
but is now mostly gray moss
with chips of white sticking up
like shattered headstones.

"Beatrix, look."
Claudia points to
a column with
burns on it.
"I don't think
it's just
age that broke
this place."

I nod
seeing more burns,
more gashes in the marble
from swords or claws
or other wicked weapons.

We continue
through the dull
black marble entrance.
It looks like it was once a clone
of Ephram's library.

But now, it is old,
forgotten,
neglected.

Claudia steps away from me,
hiding at the entrance opening wall.
She squeezes the meditation mat
and nods to me.

Inside the temple is complete dark.

Holding the fork with both hands
I take a deep breath
and go in.

Alone.

As planned.

Feeling my light within,
I push it out
glowing
to light my way
into the temple's dark heart.

I have what I always wanted,
to be alone, but now,
there's nothing I need more
than Claudia's help.

Her bravery.

Her confidence.

I go forward
alone.

Chapter 9

Sanctum Sanctorum

Columns line the interior
of the temple.
Once they were white marble
with gold veins;
now they are yellowed
and dulled with scars.

Holding the fork close,
slowly I walk to the center
of the temple
where a statue stands
of a cloaked man.
It looks like Ephram,
holding a shield over his head.

Stains on the statue,
where water once flowed,
cascade down like an
ancient fountain.

"It was."
Shadow and
razor thin broken glass arms
strut out from behind
a column into
my light.
"The water came out
and ran down the shield
like a dome.
Representing the Veil."

Wall my thoughts.
Brick by brick.

The necklace glints
in my light
screaming for me
to notice it
to want it.

And I do.

I do want it.

Just to touch it.

"You found more for me?"
the book asks.
"More of what you call
energy?"

"Is it not?"
Wall my thoughts.

Placing bricks in my mind
in a flurry of mental motion.

Claudia's moving around me
by now
sticking to the shadows.

Wall my thoughts.
"What is it if not energy?"

> "Reality is more than
> matter and energy.
> You call it energy,
> others call it magic,
> Brother Ephram would have
> called it
> Aether."
> It slithers closer to me
> breaking into my light
> pressing the necklace
> to my face.
>
> "Were you holding out on me?"
> It laughs
> and runs a talon up
> my throat
> pushing up my chin.
> "I wanted it all.
> Thought I had it."

"I guess I'm full
of surprises."
Wall my thoughts.
Smearing grout between the bricks
black smoke leaks through;
I close the holes in my mind.

I circle the fountain,
looking for Claudia.

She's coming.

She didn't leave me.
No.
She didn't.

"Did she leave you?"
the shadow says.
Damn!
Wall my thoughts.
"She died. She left you.
Everyone leaves you,
Beatrix."

No, she'll come.

She just needs a moment.
Wall my thoughts.

"What happens when the Veil comes down?"
I press the fork toward it.

"Then my family is free
and we are free to avenge
our banishment."

422

"Revenge on the Brothers of Clmal?"
My eyes jut in the dark
for Claudia.

"Oh, no."
It chuckles
the noise rippling
around me.

The black hole
in the galaxy of its eye
spasms in delight.
"They bound us to the Veil,
but others exiled us from
our home.
Our vengeance
shall be upon them."

It rushes around me.
I spin, keeping the fork
between us.

"Did you think humans
were capable of keeping us
from home?"
It gurgles a laugh.
"Humans!? You cannot
even perceive what is beyond
the Veil, beyond the Rim.
True power lies out there.

And I will have it."

Claudia nods from the shadows
and I stab into the spiral galaxy eye
with the Fork of Binding.

Claudia leaps over me
jumping from the fountain
stretching the meditation mat
to wrap up the smoke and creature within.

Chanting the binding spell
as I thrust it at the creature
my arms stop mid-stab.
The fork swings off target
as the broken glass arms
grab my strands.

I wasn't paying attention.

It has been gathering my strands,
my pink lightning flailing wildly about,
since it rushed to me.
The necklace
was a distraction.

A claw stretches up grabbing Claudia
in the air
and rips away the meditation mat.
It strangles her
as she kicks and flails.

It bellows a laugh.
"Look familiar, you two?"
Strangling Claudia,
draining me.
"Both of you have been here
before!"

I stab again at it
but the fork is ripped away
clanging over the marble floor.

No!

The mat floats away
colliding with a column
far away from us.

I reach to grab the smoke
remembering the scene
over Ephram and Claudia's bodies,
the advice the book gave me
to destroy the red smoke.

It shoves me away.
Holding me by the strings
a broken puppet being drained
of life.

"Not this time."

Claudia grips her ice axes
and swings into the smoke
hitting nothing.

It strangles her.

It drains me.

                     "Beatrix!"
                     Claudia screams
                     over me
                     the three talons cutting away
                     her air.
                     "We're not done!"
                     Her throat clenches.

We.

We are not done.

I swing my hands up
to grab her
but she kicks
at the broken glass arm
holding her
and I can't get her foot.

"Foot!"

Reaching up
catching shoestrings.

I shout to her mind
thinking of only her mind.
When I get your foot,
imagine you're pulling
energy from the monster!
Her foot drops
and I grab it
as the smoke throws us
to the side.

"As I said, not this time."
It laughs as we crawl to get up.

We clatter on the floor
rolling to where the mat fell,
the tuning fork steps away.

The smoke glows
with what it stole from me.
It took enough for
whatever it's about to do.

The three finger claws
coil around the statue
constricting it
cracking it
releasing gurgling
bubbling
molten light
pooling at the tripod leg
holding the black smoke upright.

Puffing up the smoke expands
and snaps down on the
statue,
crunching
shattering the stone
sending the white liquid light
into a spraying shower
exploding into the air.

That's the same light
from the wound in the world
at the stone circle…?

The same that was
slobbering out of me
when I was drained dry.

Drops of glowing white light
rain down over the black smoke,
the rippling void of black space,
purple nebula scar, and stars,
distorting it like
steam in an ice storm.

"Get the mat,"
I say to Claudia.

She's choking
to get breath back in her lungs.

She nods quickly
and scurries to it.

The smoke puffs up again,
glowing brighter,
and squeezes again
another crack to the fountain
spraying more of the
viscus glowing liquid.

From all around us
a ripping sound sets
every hair on edge,
goosebumps erupting over my body.

Claudia stops
looking for the sound
worry surfacing on her face,
tugging her shoulders down.

It's the same ripping sound
from the stone circle
but this time so loud,
so deep,
it isn't a door,
it's a grand gate
for the things in the Veil
to parade out in victory,
liberated.

Reality was just torn apart.

I look to find the opening,
but I don't see it.
The rip, the wound in the world
isn't here...?

                              "Freedom!"
                              it screams.
                              Contracting again
                              breaking the statue
                              exploding the fountain
                              making it rain
                              inside the temple.

Water pools around the smoke,
drenching the remains of the statue.

"Hey!"
The spiral galaxy eye
narrows on me.
I step outside the puddle
forming from the fountain.

Claudia still running to the mat
outside the rain.
"Just like electricity!"

Holding up the tarot card
I pulled from my pocket,
The Chariot,
I drop it outside the growing pool
from the fountain.

Hitting the water
with the Fork of Binding,
chanting the words,
seeing the purple
bolts of light
erupt from the fork
and swirl into the white liquid
rising up and around
the black smoke.

The broken glass arms and leg
claw into the marble floor,
writhing and ripping away
from the purple strands
entangling them
flexing around the smoke body,
lancing through the black hole
in the spiral galaxy eye.

I chant louder
feeling the energy in me
focusing through the fork.

Feeling the cookie
in my gut
grow and surge.

"Just like electricity.
Current travels through water, jackass."

"The Veil is open!"
the black hole warbles
stretching and collapsing,
screaming
in defiance.
"You will be devoured."

"Not by you."
I pull the fork from the glowing water
and tap the card
sending a staggering

BOOONNNNNGGGG

throughout the temple.

Claudia grabs her ears,
stumbling back from the shockwave.
The wave sucks me in
throwing me against
the fountain remains
and toppling over it.

The stone statue falls as I hit it
unleashing a geyser of thick light.
I tumble through it
rolling to the ground.

Claudia runs to me,
checks me,
our eyes going to the card.

It is still.

I get up
and see the necklace
lying on the floor,
glittering in my faint
but growing light.

I go to it.

Seeing the blue metal
and gold chains
sprawled on the floor.

I sigh,
listening
for the thing that was in the book,
now in the card.

Hearing

nothing.

A gurgle of
whispers
fades quickly

to

silence.

Turning back,
seeing Claudia watch me,
I smile and turn from the necklace.

The Gate

Claudia runs to the entrance.

I look at the statue
now rubble.
How are we going
to fix this?

        "Beatrix! You need to see this!"
        Claudia screams.
        Panic flooding her.

I run out to her,
following her gaze up into
the cosmic sky
and see the nebula's
gaping chasm slobbering out
white liquid light.

What was green nebula gasses are now
boiling blisters
festering and busting open
spraying white light
in geysers through the
starry black sky.

The Veil is open
for any to escape.

The rippling flesh inside,
the guts of reality flexing and stretching
as the creatures,
the Lightless,
flee their prison.

So many of them.
Smoke bodies gush from
the wound...no, not a wound,
wound doesn't scale
to this laceration in reality,
the flesh of this world
gouged and stretched open
as horrid things wriggle out
screaming and wailing in freedom's delight.

"What now?"
I breathe.

Claudia's response
is an empty stare
at the gaping hole
in the green gasses
streaking the sky.

"How do you even fix this!?"
I scream.

                              "How'd you do it before?"
                              Claudia asks.
                              "When the book tricked you?"

"I didn't fix it.
Ephram did."

                              "What about the other time?"

"The black smoke
redirected my power
to absorb it."
I look back to the fountain.

The surging glowing liquid
spraying up.

I run to it,
looking through the volcano of light
feeling the frozen cold
of it.

I look harder,
plucking a silver string
projecting a force
to part the water
down to see
a shaft of light.

"How'd you do that?"

"New trick."
I shrug,
thoughts of Quinn and how
shocked she'd be right now
springing to mind.

I push it away
letting out a little chuckle
to distract me from how bad
things are.

My bad feeling was right.

"Look."
Pointing to the liquid.
"It's magic energy."

Maybe something like a wire
carrying the energy to maintain
the Veil?

"If the Veil is breaking
because it isn't getting enough current,
like electricity,
then I just need to close the circuit."

Looking to the broken statue,
I see where the base
covered this opening.

The statue kept the flow contained
and with the statue broken,
the energy isn't contained.

I bet the fountain
was a pressure valve
to release excess energy
that had built up over time.

But now's not the time
to mentally reconstruct
ancient magical artifacts.

"I've got to seal it up!"

                              "What can I do!?"
                              Claudia yells
                              as a warbling roar
                              comes from the entrance.

A pyramid head creature's
massive three-armed body
shifts through the temple entrance.

It's one of the things
that killed Mike,
almost killed me.

Ephram called it a
pyradente.

"Never mind. I've got this.
You do that."

Claudia grabs her axes
and rushes at the beast.

I take a deep breath
and look for the strings,
those silver strands
I just saw.

Another breath.

They begin to appear
drifting up from the opening
like seaweed.

I grab them
and start stitching the
strands of seaweed together
feeling the frozen white liquid
bubbling out,
drenching my hands,
pulling on my energy.

Dropping the seaweed strands.
Flicking the white light liquid
from my hands.

Realization sets in.
This is going to drain me.

Maybe forever.

Claudia buries her axe
into the beast's face,
at least I think that's its face.

Another one
comes through the door.

I need to help her.

Looking down at the strands,
the white light
spraying up from the reservoir below,
I plunge my hands in and
think of the cookie.

Nothing can take my power.

I stitch
and twist and wrap
tying and knotting.

Draining energy from me
the white light pulls harder
than anything I've met so far.
Not greedy,
just drinking
like a mindless machine
consuming the necessary energy
to continue operation.

The glowing liquid
numbs my fingers
and I shake them
to thaw them
so they can work
their deft knotting.

Tense straining tendons
scream in pain
as my fingers tire
from the tiny knots.

Shaking my hands hard
to bring back feeling,
to throw off the pain
locking my fingers
in a knuckle chain of
stiffening paralysis.

"It's working!"
Claudia screams from
the entrance of the temple.

When did she go there?
"It's closing!"
She points up
outside the temple.
Blue slime is splashed
all over her and
drips freely from
her axes.

I keep tying
shaking life back into my fingers
on one hand as the other
screams, freezes, holds
my work together.

Vision getting blurry.

I dig in,
remembering the cookie,
thinking of the cookie,
glowing now,
surging pink to purple
as I stitch and twist.

My light tinting
the white liquid pink.
The spouting
reduced to leaking
tied off to
gurgling.

GAH!
A noose catches my throat
ripping me back
feeling slicing wires
across my throat.

One of those beasts got through
and now it's eating my energy.
I'm fading.

Dimming.

The cookie!

I can't find it.

Stitching faster
closing the gurgling
tying off the last leak
as the beast closes in.

Mouth opening
teeth buzz-sawing around the pyramid head
as it lurches toward me with its arms
stretched.

The wire is sealed with a humming
radiating blazing white light
blinding me,
blinding the beast.
It shrieks,
stumbling back
as I get to my feet.

Deep breath.

The cookie is back.

I reach out my fingers
and flick one of the many silver strands
that surround me.

So many can be seen...
how did I miss them before?

WOOHHHMMMM!!!

Energy explodes from the strand
evaporating the beast
into a haze of faint
gray snow.

Another pyradente
races toward me.
I brace to strike
as an axe tip explodes through
its chest
followed by a geyser
of chunky blue slime.
It drops to the ground
revealing Claudia standing behind it.

> "The rip is closed,"
> Claudia pants.

Her body painted with
the blue blood
of the countless
bodies I'm just now
noticing all around me.

> "We need to get out of here.
> They know we're here,"
> she says.

"I saw more coming,
and some smoke too."

"Well, then let's get going."
I grab the necklace
throw it in my bag
and hand it to her.
"Can you carry that?"

"And these?"
She opens my bag
showing the books
I brought from
Ephram's library.

"Keep them."
I nod.
"We have a lot of learning to do."

"Can we leave that
open like that?"
Claudia points
to the white light
radiating from an open hole
in the ground.

Going to the rubble,
she and I push the statue's remains
and other rocks into the hole.

"Will that hold?"
she doubts.

I shrug,
uncertain.

"We'll fix it better
later.
Gotta figure out how
first."

                              "Will it stay sealed?"
                              Claudia watches the entrance.

Howls and screeches
come from farther away.

I shake my head.
"I don't know but
I think you need a lot of power
to mess with this."

Shifting through my bag
for the book we need right now.
"The creature in the book
said it needed me
to do this.

I think it will be okay
until we come back."

Claudia nods
and rolls her ice axe
to encourage me to hurry.

Pulling out *The Book of Doors*,
I flip to the page on summoning the door
back to the library.

Plucking the strands around me,

the purple doorknob emerges from nowhere
as the black door's odd angles take shape.

The door swings open.

"The Library of Clmal."

"The Library of Clmal."

We walk through.

Claudia Bain

Burials

A shovel is in the Garden.

I dig for hours while Beatrix
reads in the library.
She comes out to check on me
a few times
but I thought this a task
better done alone.

Once deep enough,
I roll Ephram in.
The mud beside the library
gives easily to digging
and welcomes his body
with a soft thud.

Climbing down with him,
I turn him face up
to watch the cosmic sky
in a peaceful eternal night.

My eyes drift to the fantastic sites
that constantly hang over us,
sites I've never taken a moment
to appreciate.

This place is beautiful.
From the black trees
to the shattered blue planet
and the golden veined library
in front of which I am burying Ephram.

"Thank you."
I place the blue teapot
in his hands.
"I'm ready for new tea."

I nod.

Tea splashes in the teapot.

Climbing out of Ephram's resting place,
I shovel the soft soil over him,
dropping in some seeds from
his tea boxes.

"Master Oni told me
a great teacher can be forgotten
but the lessons will never be."

Shoveling more dirt,
patting it down as I go.

"I won't forget you.
Or what you gave me."

Pausing, remembering the
burning bitter tea
ending with the
drops of honey he left
in the cup for me.

In the end,
after the
scalding heat and
bitter taste,
it was sweet.

And the sweetness lingers
far longer than the bitterness burns.

"Jasmine tea."
I nod.

Finishing the last shovel of dirt,
patting it gently,
a tear slips onto the soil.

A white star flower
twists up and blooms
where the tear fell.

I smile.
"Goodbye."

Beatrix Clark

Core World: Home

We bury Ephram outside the library
where he saved us
the first time.

He tried to save us
so many times
and eventually,
he did.

His books.

His tea.

His hope.

Claudia burns Dr. Roderick's clothes
and leaves them near the black forest
for whatever might find them
tasty.

Inside the library,
we search for other stories
of other books
that were bound with spirits like
The Garden and The Well.

We find a few references to a book
left on our world decades ago
in Glen Coast, Maryland.

                        "I can't believe this book
                        caused all this trouble."
                        Claudia flips through
                        The Garden and The Well.

"Books will do that."
I chuckle.
"Why do you think
they are banned,
burned,
boycotted?"

People would rather ban a book
than a gun because one
can kill,
the other
can transform.

To some,
death is easier,
less terrifying.

Claudia hands me back
the book that started all this
and searches for other books.

"What are you looking for?"

"Ephram said,
'know thy enemy.'
I'm looking for some help
to defeat the Lightless."
She sighs.
"I don't think we're done yet."

She goes to the Altar of Clmal
and brings the book there
and asks if I'd read it
to her.

Why can't she read this?

Why can I?

I nod and smile,
seeing this is important to her.

We look for more and eventually
realize we'll always find more
reasons to keep looking.

So, we pack what we can,
and head to the Room of Doors.

"Ready?"

The white door,
gold handle is
ready for us
to go home.

She nods.
"You saved us Beatrix."

"No, I just-"

"I saw you with the necklace,
at the end.
You chose us
over what it could do for you."

"It wasn't a choice."
I smile.
"It...wasn't an easy choice."
Truth humbling me.

I wanted to be done.

I wanted to just walk away
but in the end,
I wanted that feeling again.

The feeling of power,
of I don't care,
of I can do anything,
of I can be anyone.

"*You* saved us."
I nod.

"Mac and cheese on me."
She laughs.

I grimace.

"Quinn would be so proud of you,
Trixie."
She smirks wily,
fun breathed back into her.

"Trixie?"

Could be worse.
But I'm not just my tricks.
This power flowing through me
isn't a trick.
It's not a toy.

It is deadly.

I roll my eyes at the name.
"Beatrix is fine."
I wink.
"Can we just avoid Quinn
and any clubs
for a while?"

Remembering Mike,
we both grin
through his loss.
We didn't know him,
but he was nice,
seemed like a good person.

"I think we have too much
reading to do for any nights out
anytime soon."
Claudia nods
to the bag with the books.
"Ephram said to leave this one."

She pulls out
The Book of Doors.
I push it back in.
"We'll need it.
We've got a lot to do
back home.

If these books are right,
the Lightless won't stop here.
We've got to find a way
to stop them."

Claudia nods and looks back to the bag,
her eyes tracing the tarot card,
the Chariot.

She looks at me.
I smile to dismiss her concerns
looking back to the door
to escape her eyes.

Twisting the handle,
the door opens
and we both say,

"Apartment."

Epilogue

Weeks Later...

Beatrix Clark

Brrr...

Brrr...

"Hello?"

I sniff in the
smell of lavender
from my perfume.

"Hi Mom!
How are you today?"

                    "Beatrix?
                    You know what time it is?"
                    Mom yawns
                    and it hits me.

"Oh, sorry Mom.
Time zones and all."
I laugh.
"I got you a beer stein."

                    "I don't drink?"
                    She chuckles.

"No, but it's good for iced tea too!"
I heft up the glass
thinking this will be perfect
chilled with Mom's Kentucky sweet tea.

The tea that makes your teeth vibrate
from all the sugar.

                    "Hey, Beatrix,
                    time to roll!"
                    Claudia calls over my shoulder.
                    "Hi Mrs. Clark!"

                    "Where are you?"
                    Mom shouts
                    holding back a laugh.
                    "Sounds loud."

I look at the rock club around me
and it is loud.
The band is screaming in German
and the drums are driving.

Who knows what they're saying,
it's just grunts and growls.

"Berlin in Germany.
Remember, I told you
I was going to-"

                              "Yes, Germany, I remember
                              but why is it so loud?"
                              Mom laughs.

It's good to hear her laugh.
Makes me feel
lighter.

"We're at a nightclub.
Trendy place."
I follow quickly with,
"Don't worry, I'm with Claudia."

                              "Good. She needs to
                              rub off on you.
                              Get you out of your room."
                              Mom smiles.

                              "Beatrix, let's roll!"
                              Claudia holds up her wrist
                              and duffle bags
                              tapping the universal
                              'time to go' sign.

"Gotta go Mom!
Love you!"

"Wait!"
Mom shouts.
"You know the rules,
where are you going?"

She pauses.
"I don't mind the globetrotting
but I need to know where you are.
It's a mom thing."

"Ugh...fine.
We're heading to Egypt."
Claudia gives me a serious look.
"Pyramid sight-seeing."

"Take lots of pictures.
I love you honey.
Be safe."

I pause on that last one.

"Safe as I can be."
I giggle
nervously.

I hang up.

"Egypt?"
Claudia asks
handing me my duffle.

"I can't tell her
where we're really going."
The mass of our trip
weighing on me.

Be safe,
Mom said.

I don't think
that's possible
this time.

"Going to a small town
isn't so terrible,"
Claudia says,
pushing her ice axe
deeper into her duffle.

"This one is,"
I say.

"Why are we flying?
Can't we just,
you know..."
She mimes opening a door.

"Doors don't get there,"
I sigh.

"Oh..."
All humor dies
on her face.
"That kind of place.

We step out of the club
to a starry night
in Berlin.

An empty night.

A quiet night.

"Abbots Manor."

Author's Note

I hope you enjoyed Library of Lessons & Lies. As stated in the Introduction, this story first showed up in the late 90s and hasn't gone away since. In fact, quite the opposite. This story has bloomed into a massive tale that's been cooking in me for decades now. At times it feels like all my stories are just offshoots of this tale.

If you have not read [dis]connection or BLOTS, I'd encourage you to do so. If you're wondering where Abbots Manor is, that's answered in BLOTS. In this series' next book, we'll explore that town and make a brief stop in Glen Coast, MD - the setting of [dis]connection. There are other places connected in this story, other people, and I hope you enjoy discovering the dots.

Originally this book was titled BIBLIOPHILE but as the series started forming in my mind, that word was better for the series as we'll encounter many book lovers throughout Beatrix & Claudia's journey. Two of those book lovers are in BLOTS but you'll find out more about them as you read on in the series.

In the next book we'll be learning more about Claudia and her family. We'll meet some of the people she's been trying to escape and learn a lot more about Beatrix's power as well. I hope we see you there. Sign up for my newsletter to keep informed when new BIBLIOPHILE stories come online.

But before we go from this tale, let's find out what happened to one of the characters who's story is just beginning...

"Hello?"

"Hello!?" His voice echoes back angrier as it returns. Looking over the ruin of this place, he kneels to a crumble of rock in the center of the columns.

He thinks maybe once upon a time, this place was a temple. Once it had a ceiling that hid the stars and nebula above. But now, this place is destroyed. It is ruin, scarred with the memories of battles long ago, and perhaps a battle more recently.

Lifting a large stone from the rubble, the man orients the sculpture and sees what it was. A shield. It's heavy. The man drops it. The shield cracks.

"Oh…" He springs up. "Oh no." He panics, pressing the pieces back together.

"That will not help," a voice booms from the darkness.

The man who broke the shield stands and startles toward the voice. "I'm just looking. I'm lost," he says.

"You are lost because you wander to a place you do not belong." Another man, this one in a flowing purple robe, emerges from the shadow of a broken column. The robe's golden threading lights up the shadows with warm, electric light. A shimmering gold crown of light wreathes his head and rises to wavering spikes, matching his thin white beard.

"No, I was tricked," the man at the rubble says. He brushes off his jeans feeling the immediate need to look his best. But the mud on his pants won't come off, nor will the blood on his shirt. "I was tricked by…" His cheeks redden, almost blending into his tight curls of ginger hair. "I was tricked by a book." He sighs.

"Many have been. And yet, you live." The man's purple robe flows around him with a quiet swish as he glides over the floor to the rubble. "How have you survived the machinations of the Lightless?" He chuckles. "Of the ancient Lost Brother Mot of Ugarit?" Raising his long ancient finger to his glowing crown, the purple robed man squints at the bloody shirt, dirty jeans, finding the man's name in his mind. "Russel…Dr. Russel Carlton, how did you survive?"

Russ feels the man in his mind and knows the time of truth has come. "We made a deal." Russ's hand flies toward the purple cloak, feeling the lifeforce within that cloak. Smiling, hungry, and ready to feast, Russ rips the lifeforce from the man. The purple cloak billows down to the ground, empty of the life that was once within. A stench of death is released into the air, leaving the mark of The Dark Craft for anyone who wanders here.

Kicking the rocks to the side, Russ sees a beam of white light leak out of rubble. He smiles, remembering what he learned from the thing in the book. The promises made if he held up his end of the deal. Russ knew Greg got the book and knew he came here.

The Garden is growing. And Russ wants to be the Gardener. The book said he could. He bends down and replaces the rocks covering the white light.

"Just a few more things." Russ nods. "Now I know you're here. Just a few more things to find and I'll be back." He shivers, thinking about the boy who told him about the book. The boy in the street who was waiting for him. Shaking away the feeling that accompanied thoughts of the boy, Russ returns to the task at hand.

The boy…Russ has tried not to think of him. Even here on the Rim, Russ knows merely thinking of the boy could call him. And if thoughts of the boy bring chills and screams to his mind, the boy appearing would be truly horrible. Best to keep his thoughts on the task at hand, not the boy.

Russ convulses to escape the thoughts of that kid and thinks about the things he needs.

A book.

A sword.

A coin.

A scepter.

A hammer.

And where can he find these things, he wonders. Well, in the one place you find all knowledge. In the Library. He shoves his hands in his pockets, smiles, and leaves the Temple of the Veil whistling "Somewhere Over the Rainbow."

Stay Connected

Hey, Tim here. I hope you enjoyed *Library of Lessons and Lies*. This is Book One of the Bibliophile series. While Beatrix and Claudia have a long path ahead of them, they are not the only adventurers journeying through the Core Worlds, the Rim, and the Dreamlands (you'll find that in *[dis]connection*).

Subscribe to my newsletter to keep up with all the happenings, including free stories released to newsletter subscribers first.

https://timkulp.com/library-lessons-lies

See you around!

Tim

She made a monster, now, can she stop it?

Erin's the new girl at Glen Coast High School. Her passion for technology makes her an outcast in this small town community. She's friendless and bullied until she finds an experimental 3d printer that lets her create a friend, just not a human friend. When her creation turns violent, Erin must connect with family and friends before her creation takes everything, including her life.

See why readers are calling [dis]connection "Addictive", "Frankenstein for the Social Network Generation" and "a memorable young adult novel in both substance and style."

Tech, myth and magic collide in this novel-in-verse perfect for teens looking to mix horror, technology and modern life with Social Media. Teens who love to code will love how coding is mixed with verse to tell Erin's story.

Can Erin save her family from the horror she has created? Or will the ultimate secret of the Pandora Project rip Erin apart before her creation has a chance?

Available Now at

https://timkulp.com/books/disconnection

More Bibliophiles hide here...

Beatrix, Claudia and the professors are not the only people who love ancient books, or forbidden knowledge. Discover the orgins of Old Jack and Jenny Fields within the pages of BLOTS. You will see them again, very soon, in future Bibliophile tales.

See what readers are calling "CREEPTACULAR!" and "An inventive and unusual collection of horror,"

BLOTS brings you stories spanning the horror spectrum. From cosmic horror to fairy tale folk horror and gothic ghost stories, BLOTS has something for any fan of the macabre.

If you like Darcy Coates style hauntings, reimagined fairy tales or H. P. Lovecraft's exploration of the unknown, you'll love BLOTS.

Ghosts and monsters lurk in these stories. Like ink blots, some of these horrors are more than they seem. If you stare too long, you might see them, or they might see you.

Available Now at

https://timkulp.com/books/blots

About the Author

From B movies to blockbusters, Tim has a passion for horror and exploring the things that give us the shivers. Stories from authors like Poe, Lovecraft, Tolkien and King have shaped Tim's writing style with a focus on world building and monster making.

When not writing fiction, Tim is a regular contributor to technology publications on Artificial Intelligence and Virtual Reality. He's Dungeons & Dragons fanboy and enjoys life just outside of Baltimore, MD with his loving wife, amazing kids, friendly dog, and vengeful cat.

Keep up with Tim on his blog https://www.timkulp.com

CREDITS

Author: Tim Kulp

Cover Design: Thea Magerand

Editors: Linda Trout, Nicole Fegan, Roisin Heycock

General Font: Adobe Garamond Pro

Notes Font: Bradley Hand ITC

Beatrix's Font: Kristal by Eyal Holtzman

Claudia's Font: Brother 1816 by Fernando Díaz and Ignacio Corbo

Gregory Roderick's Font: Baskerville Old Face

Book's Voice: Antiquarian Scribe by Brian Willson

Book Layout: Adobe InDesign

Beams of Light image: Adobe Stock image by d1sk

Chapter Magical Symbols: Images generated by Midjourney using the following prompts:

> line art, camera view from the floor, drawing of a temple interior with pillars and stone flooring, grimy dirty old rundown --v 4

> line art, ink drawing of a black door with light spilling out of it, the door is partially open, there is nothing else in the room --v 4 --q 2

> line art, abstract sacred geometry and magic symbols, white background, black ink --v 4 --q 2